TEMPLE OF THE MOON

Gabrielle had gone to Yucatan in Central America in a last attempt to salvage her marriage-that-wasn't-a-marriage to James Warner—and immediately found herself in conflict with the disturbing Shaun Lennox. And it would be no help to any of them if she should be so foolish as to fall in love with Shaun . . .

Books you will enjoy
by SARA CRAVEN

WILD MELODY

On the strength of her brief holiday romance with Jeremy Lord, Catriona left her quiet Scottish home and came up to London to marry him. But Jeremy, of course, had forgotten all about her by now—and instead she found herself involved with his sophisticated uncle Jason. Who was even more out of her league than Jeremy had been . . .

A GIFT FOR A LION

When Joanna landed herself uninvited on the tiny, mysterious Mediterranean island of Saracina she promptly fell into the hands of its stern over-lord, Leo Vargas—which probably served her right. But the real danger facing her was not to her person but to her heart!

STRANGE ADVENTURE

Young Lacey Vernon was being more or less forced to marry the Greek tycoon Troy Andreakis to save her father from ruin—but as time went on she began to realise, unwillingly, that perhaps she wasn't dreading him as much as she had imagined she was. But that was before she learned what kind of a man Troy really was . . .

THE GARDEN OF DREAMS

Lissa wasn't quite sure whether she wanted to marry the attractive Frenchman Paul de Gue or not, so she was glad to accept his invitation to visit the family chateau in France and meet his relatives. Unfortunately, this also involved meeting the austere Comte Raoul de Gue—who made it clear that he did *not* want Lissa marrying into the family!

TEMPLE OF THE MOON

BY

SARA CRAVEN

MILLS & BOON LIMITED
17–19 FOLEY STREET
LONDON W1A 1DR

First published 1977
Philippine copyright 1977
This edition 1977

ISBN 0 263 72509 X

Set in Linotype Plantin 10 on 11pt.

Made and printed in Great Britain by
Richard Clay (The Chaucer Press), Ltd., Bungay, Suffolk

CHAPTER ONE

It had been raining for several hours, a monotonous, relentless downpour that turned the gutters into miniature torrents and transformed the once sun-baked streets into shallow canals, swirling with red dust and debris.

Gabrielle sat alone in the foyer of the Hotel Belen, her eyes fixed bleakly on the huge glass swing doors which gave on to the street. Her fingers drummed restlessly on the small carved table in front of her, keeping time with the raindrops. She felt totally alien to the laughing, chattering groups of tourists sitting around her, exclaiming over this unseasonable break in the weather pattern in what was officially the dry season in the Yucatan peninsula. Once or twice she glanced down at the camera case lying at her feet as if seeking reassurance.

She was here, she told herself, where she had every right to be, so it was ridiculous to think that this sudden rainstorm was some kind of ill-omen. Even if James was not prepared to welcome her to Merida, she still had her commission from *Vision* magazine to fulfil. She was a working woman now, whether he liked it or not. And there could be all sorts of explanations as to why he had never answered the slightly defiant letter she had sent him, telling him that *Vision* had bought some of the work she had sent them in a fit of bravado and wanted more, Perhaps he had never received the letter. After all, this was hardly the most accessible place in the world, and if James was in the depths of the Mayan forests somewhere, he would hardly be in a position to conduct a correspondence.

But the more she tried to bolster up her self-confidence, the more frankly depressed she became. Other archaeologists managed to keep in touch with their wives and families, she knew, and long silences had invariably been James' way of manifesting his displeasure with her during their brief married life. And in the past, she had always been the first to ask forgiveness, daunted by this forbidding chill, but not now, she thought. Not any more. This time, there was nothing for James to forgive. He had deliberately, almost cold-bloodedly shut her out of his career. He could not prevent her seeking one of her own, although he had made it icily clear before he had left for Mexico that he did not want a working wife.

Gabrielle sighed, and ran her fingers round the neck of her dress, lifting the collar away slightly from her throat. In spite of the air conditioning in the hotel, she found the humidity trying and she knew that in the forest regions she would have tropical conditions to contend with. But even the prospect of more discomfort could not prevent a mercurial change in her spirits at the thought of the trip ahead.

To think that she was actually going to see them—these strange ancient pyramids rising out of the jungle, evocative memorials of an advanced civilisation that had been wiped out by the Spanish conquest. For as long as she could remember, the conquest of Mexico had fascinated her, and she had read every book on the subject she could lay her hands on. Her father, who had taught at a northern university, had always encouraged her interest, although he had not shared it particularly. His own researches were based nearer home into Roman and Celtic remains, and father and daughter had amicably agreed to differ. They'd had a warm, happy relationship, made even closer by her mother's death quite unexpectedly during a minor operation. Dr Christow had aged visibly under this blow, but he had been determined not to allow it to affect Gabrielle's growing-up, and his older sister Molly, herself a widow, had come to live with them, becoming a more than adequate substitute mother as Gabrielle advanced into her teens.

Her father's death had occurred when she was halfway through a photographic course at art college, and she had immediately offered to abandon the course and get a job to help out financially, but Aunt Molly had been adamant in her refusal. Gabrielle might well be glad of some qualifications one day, she had insisted, although she had no means of knowing how right she would be.

Gabrielle had been at the end of her course when she met James. She had seen his lecture on ancient Aztec civilisations advertised at the local adult education centre and had recognised in the Dr James Warner with the impressive string of letters after his name the Jimmy Warner who had been at university with her father and worked with him on digs in their younger days.

When the lecture was over, she nerved herself to approach him and explain who she was. James Warner was a slightly built man, with severely cut greying hair and a trim beard, and in her wildest dreams Gabrielle could not envisage anyone, even her extrovert father, calling him 'Jimmy', but he had greeted her with every appearance of delight and asked her to stay on and have coffee with him.

Her initial reservations had soon been swept away by his evident affection for her father and distress at the news of his death.

'I was abroad, of course, when it happened,' he told her. 'By the time I heard about it, I felt it was too late even to write and offer my condolences. I had no idea Charles had a daughter, either.'

He drove her back to her digs after the lecture and said they must keep in touch, but it was a vague remark and Gabrielle did not really expect to hear from him again, although she thought regretfully that she would have liked more time with him to give her a chance to ask more things about ancient Mexico that did not come within the normal scope of a lecture.

But to her surprise, she did hear from him again, and

quickly. He wrote to her, and followed this up with a telephone call and flowers. He had several speaking engagements in the neighbourhood and invited Gabrielle to go to these as his guest. It was useless to pretend she was not flattered by his attentions and in many ways she felt as safe with James as she had with her father, although the two men were not a bit alike and she knew it.

At first she told herself that James' kindness to her was prompted solely by the fact that she was her father's daughter, but as time went by, she began to realise this was not the whole truth. His wooing might have begun cautiously, but soon there was no doubt of his intentions. James wanted to marry her. He told her so one evening when they were dining together before going to the theatre. He spoke frankly on the considerable difference in their ages and on his previous marriage which had ended in divorce some years previously.

'My former wife could not accept the demands that my work made on my time,' he said. 'She had no interest in my researches and hated travelling. Whereas you, my dear Gabrielle, share my fascination with the Maya. You could be a great help to me—even an inspiration.'

If Gabrielle hesitated at all, it was only momentarily, and if an inner voice warned her to make sure she was attracted by the man and not merely by the life he could offer her, she hushed it. She had been oddly touched too by James' old-fashioned ideas of courtship and his evident respect for her innocence. She had been disturbed by the permissive behaviour that seemed to be the pattern at the college she had attended and her determination to stay apart from it had resulted in her being called a prig, and even more unkindly a professional virgin by some of the other students. The labels had stuck and in spite of the attractions of her dark copper hair and green eyes, fringed by long lashes, she had spent a rather lonely existence during her student years.

Even when they were engaged, James made no attempt to push their relationship to a more intimate level, and she was grateful to him for this. The only souring of her happiness came with Aunt Molly's overt disapproval.

'Are you quite sure what you're doing, child?' she had said abruptly one day, watching Gabrielle packing some of the books she had decided to take with her to her new home. 'He's a middle-aged man, and set in his ways, and you're so young . . . Sometimes I feel so worried.'

Gabrielle sat back on her heels and looked at her aunt wide-eyed. 'But, Aunt Molly, surely you've known James for years.'

'Oh yes, I've known him all right,' her aunt reorted rather grimly. 'And that just increases my misgivings. Even your father used to say there was a side to James that no one would ever know, and that it was probably just as well. Oh, it's not just the fact that he's so much older than you, although that does disturb me too. I just wish you'd wait for a while—get to know each other a little more.'

'Oh, Aunt Molly!' Gabrielle curbed her exasperation. 'Haven't you said time and time again that no one really knows anyone until they have to live with them?'

'Yes, I have,' her aunt returned. 'And if that was all you and James wanted to do, I'd feel much happier about the whole thing.'

'I'm shocked,' Gabrielle said with an attempt at lightness. 'But seriously, can you imagine James agreeing to anything as—swinging as a trial marriage?'

They laughed together, but their amusement was forced and Gabrielle was relieved when the conversation turned to another, less personal subject. Aunt Molly was a dear, but her views of marriage were as old-fashioned in their way as James'. She believed in romance, and that love would win the day, whereas Gabrielle was convinced that marriage was a relationship demanding toleration and hard work on both sides if it was to succeed. She had been prepared to work at her marriage. What she had failed to do was ask herself if James was prepared to do the same.

Gabrielle gave a little sigh and signalled to a passing waiter. '*Quisiera una horchata, por favor,*' she said haltingly, indicating the few drops of the pale almond and rice drink remaining in her glass so that there would be no misunderstanding.

This was not how she had imagined her introduction to Mexico would be, sitting alone in a hotel foyer. She had thought James would be with her, advising her on what to order, encouraging her to use her Spanish, so painfully acquired in the comparatively brief period before she set out on her journey. But James had not even been there to meet her at the airport. Again, she had tried to make excuses for him, blaming the unreliability of the postal system, but at the same time something told her that even if one of her letters had in fact gone astray, it was unlikely that two would have done so.

She had tried very hard with the second letter. There was no note of triumph in her announcement that *Vision* had decided to send her to the Yucatan to accompany the expedition of which James was a member. She had acknowledged that she was going against his expressed wishes, first in accepting full-time employment, and again in following him to Mexico, but she had begged him to understand that she needed more from life than to spend every day sitting in that immaculate flat, watching the housekeeper Mrs Hutchinson tending the pottery and figurines so strikingly displayed in showcases and alcoves. Gabrielle had not visited James' home before their wedding, but when they returned there after the honeymoon. she was immediately conscious of a feeling of oppression. It was all so beautiful and tasteful—and slightly unreal. She had imagined she would be able to stamp something of her own personality on their home, but it had soon been made clear to her that there was no room for the sort of improvement that she visualised. Her tentative suggestion that the living room furniture could be re-grouped to provide a more homely effect had been greeted by James with a kind of horrified amusement. Gabrielle sometimes felt like a ghost. If she was merely sitting in a chair reading, and left the room momentarily, she found the cushions had been plumped up in her absence. Not even her own bedroom seemed to belong to her.

The waiter arrived with her drink and she paid him and murmured her thanks.

She had always known that there was more affection than passion in her feelings for James, but she had never intended that their marriage should be anything other than a normal one. She had been shocked and hurt to discover that James seemed in no hurry at all to consummate their relationship. At first, she had felt she ought to be grateful for his consideration—he had told her that he felt they should take time to become mentally attuned to each other before they became lovers in the physical sense—but as time went on Gabrielle felt growing doubts that James had ever wanted a wife in the real sense at all. And far from becoming mentally attuned, they seemed to be growing apart.

She had assumed that as his wife, she would be expected to take part in a certain amount of socialising. That he would have colleagues to entertain and that she would act as his hostess as she had sometimes done for her father. But they saw no one. James went each day to the Institute of Central American Studies and she was left entirely to her own devices. In the evening he read or worked in his study while she sat alone watching television.

Once and only once she had suggested that they might do some entertaining. His face had taken on the frozen look she had come to dread. 'When I wish my privacy to be invaded by a chattering horde of strangers, I'll tell you, Gabrielle.'

In spite of his unspoken disapproval, Gabrielle had invited Aunt Molly to visit her, but her aunt had not been nearly so reticent.

'Good heavens, child, it's like living in a museum!' She walked over to one of the showcases and inspected its contents with raised eyebrows. 'It must cost James a fortune in insurance. Some of these things are incredibly valuable.' She swung round and looked her niece over with a touch of grimness. 'And what are you, exactly? The latest addition to his collection?'

Gabrielle had naturally protested, but Aunt Molly's words had stayed in her memory.

The greatest disappointment of all had been James' refusal to let her take part in any of his work. During their courtship he had patiently answered all her eager questions. Now she was made to see that her curiosity was a nuisance to him, and that she interrupted his concentration.

He was busy, she told herself, but when all this paperwork was behind him and he began to prepare for the real work—for the expedition to the Yaxchilan region that she knew was brewing, then he would need her. Perhaps when they were actually in the Yucatan her enthusiasm would be the inspiration that he had once spoken of, instead of the irritation it now seemed.

She could hardly believe it when she learned that he was going without her.

'But you'll be gone for months,' she had burst out. 'You can't mean to leave me here alone. What will I do?'

He stared at her. 'Do? Occupy yourself in the same way as other wives, I imagine. You have the flat to run and . . .'

'The flat!' Gabrielle's voice was contemptuous. 'Mrs Hutchinson runs the flat and you know it. I'm not even allowed to so much as boil an egg on that immaculate stove of hers.'

James looked a little flustered and murmured something about 'female squabbles'.

'James,' she put her hand on his arm, trying not to notice

his almost instinctive withdrawal, 'please let me come with you. I've always dreamed of going to the Yucatan—you know that. Besides,' she flushed, 'we are supposed to be—getting to know one another better. How can we do that if we're thousands of miles apart?'

James made an irritable exclamation. 'Why is it women can never understand that a man's work and his personal relationships must be kept separate?' he asked in martyred tones.

'I accept that—or at least I accept that's the way you feel about it,' Gabrielle said desperately. 'But you said once that I could be—an inspiration to you. Was that just words, or did you really mean it?'

'Of course I meant it.' James sighed. 'And you are an inspiration to me, my dear. From the moment I saw you, I knew you were the one woman whose beauty would complement the setting I'd devised here. The rain forest——' he frowned and shook his head. 'That wouldn't do at all.'

'Why not?' Gabrielle asked bitterly. 'Are you afraid the goddess might come down off her pedestal and behave like a real woman after all? That I might get hot and dirty, and covered in leeches and insect bites like other human beings? I know what's involved, James, and I'm prepared to accept it if it means I can stand just for a moment on the pyramid of the Sun at Palenque, or look down into the sacred well at Chichen Itza.' She ended on a note of appeal.

'Well, I'm not prepared to accept it,' James said flatly. 'Nor am I prepared to argue about this any more. I've made my wishes clear, I think. There's nothing further to discuss.'

Up to the day of his departure, she had hoped secretly that he might relent—suggest that she joined him later, but she should have known better. His goodbyes to her were almost abstracted, as if his mind had gone ahead of him to that violent and beautiful land where stone ruins stood deserted and forgotten among the towering trees.

His letters when they came were brief, containing none of the detail or description she hungered for. All she had learned was that the expedition which was being led by a Professor Morgan was based at the Institute's headquarters in Merida, the capital of the Yucatan, and that her own letters should be directed there.

But she could not occupy every minute of the endless day in writing to James. She wasn't even sure that her letters were wanted or that her small items of news would hold any interest for him.

Photography had been her salvation. She had wandered through London, enjoying the summer weather and recording her impressions on film more for her own amusement than with any commercial intention. There was a tiny boxroom at the flat, as immaculately neat and sterile as the other rooms, and Gabrielle turned this into a temporary darkroom, ignoring Mrs Hutchinson's hostility to the move. One set of pictures involving children's street games had excited her, and these she had sent to *Vision*.

An invitation to meet the editor Martin Gilbert had followed and soon she was working regularly for them. It was over lunch with Martin and one of his feature writers one day that the name Yaxchilan had cropped up unexpectedly and she had said without thinking, 'The place of green trees.'

'Quite right.' Martin had sounded surprised. 'Now how did you know that?'

She tried to make her laugh sound light. 'Don't sound so surprised! The Mayan jungle happens to be one of my obsessions.' She twisted the plain gold ring on her left hand. 'That's where my husband is now, as a matter of fact.'

'Indeed?' Martin gave her a long considering look. 'I'm surprised that you're not with him—feeling as you obviously do.'

Gabrielle bent her head. 'I have my work here,' she said tonelessly. 'Perhaps I'll go another time. Anyway, you haven't explained what your interest is in the expedition?'

Martin laughed. 'Need you ask? We have our sights set on a feature—a big one. You know the sort of thing—cities where no human foot has sounded since the Maya left all those centuries ago—carving the memorial to a civilisation out of the encroaching jungle. There's always a fascination in that sort of thing, and we've been lucky enough to persuade Dennis Morgan, the man leading the expedition, to write the copy for us, so we can concentrate on the visual side.'

'It—it all sounds wonderful.' Gabrielle forced a smile. 'And a wonderful trip for someone,' she added bleakly, not noticing the speculative glance being exchanged by Martin and his companion.

When, a few weeks later, she was offered the assignment, she still could not believe it. She had convinced herself that her lack of overseas experience would count against her, and Martin told her frankly that she had not been far wrong.

'It was the fact that your husband is an actual member of the expedition that swung the balance in your favour,' he admitted. 'It gives you the sort of "in" that no one else could hope for. Besides, I like your work, and I have faith in it. Why shouldn't we take a chance on you?'

'You won't regret it.' Gabrielle could hardly contain her rising excitement. It wasn't just a tremendous professional opportunity, she had realised at once. It was also a chance—the best possible chance—to get her personal relationship with James on a proper footing. They could not continue as they were—she knew that. But it did not seem fair to come to any decision in isolation. James had to be consulted—she felt she owed him that, although she knew wryly that it was unlikely that he would have extended the same courtesy to her.

The more she thought about their marriage and the form it had taken, the more convinced she became that an annulment was the only answer. It was not a pleasant prospect, but it had to be faced. At best, it would be an honourable admission by them both that a mistake had been made and would leave them free to pursue their separate lives as if this strange, brief marriage had never existed. But if James did not agree—Gabrielle's heart sank every time she considered the possibility—then it must be made clear to him that she was not prepared to go on living this half-life with him. If their marriage was to continue, it had to be a real marriage with her own career and personal aspirations respected.

She sighed and bit her lip. It was wrong and cowardly, she told herself, to pray that James would opt for an annulment, yet if she was honest with herself she knew that to take up her life again with him, as his wife in deed as well as name, was the last thing she wanted. If he insisted that their marriage must be given a chance, she would have to concur, she thought wearily, and tried to subdue the quiver of revulsion that went through her.

She had been terrified that James would get wind of her visit and do something to prevent it, so she had persuaded Martin to notify the Institute that the party gathering in Merida was being joined by 'G. Christow' instead of 'Mrs J. Warner'. Later she had chided herself for cowardice and had made herself write to James, telling him the truth. She had been on edge ever since, in case word came from the Institute, rejecting her. In the meantime she had gone ahead blindly with her arrangements, obtaining the necessary documents, and having her smallpox vaccination renewed.

She had flown by jet from London to Mexico City and then had used one of the smaller domestic airlines to fly her to Merida. She would have preferred to travel there by train, stopping off on the way to visit the famous ruins at Palenque, but had sacrificed her own wishes under the compulsion to get to Merida and establish herself with the expedition.

One of her first actions, after taking up her reservation at the hotel, had been to write a note to Professor Morgan announcing her arrival and sending it round to the Institute. She knew they would all be busy with last-minute preparations for the trip and felt it would be better to allow the professor to contact her at his own convenience rather than arrive on the Institute doorstep, tacitly demanding attention they might not have time to give her. For the past twenty-four hours she had not dared to leave the hotel in case a message came for her, but she had been disappointed. She told herself resolutely that much of the depression she was feeling was due to jet lag—nothing more. But James' failure to meet her at the airport, followed by this chill silence from the Institute, was unnerving to say the least.

The hotel doors swung inwards, and she glanced up instinctively as she had done so many times during the course of the day. But this was no influx of wet, disgruntled tourists. It was a man, on his own, and somehow Gabrielle knew, as her casual gaze fixed and sharpened, that he was no tourist. He was tall and long-legged moving with an easy animal grace in denim shirt and pants with a matching rain-spattered jacket slung carelessly over one shoulder. He threaded his way through the chatting groups to the reception desk where a smiling clerk turned to greet him. She couldn't hear what passed between them, nor could she lip-read, but he was obviously asking a question, and Gabrielle felt a sudden, illogical trickle of apprehension along her spine as the newcomer turned, his eyes flicking almost indifferently over the tables. She sensed rather than saw the clerk reply, and knew with all the certainty of pounding heart and pulses that they were both looking at her.

She picked up her glass with fingers that shook, and took a hasty sip. Surely this couldn't be Professor Morgan? Martin had given her the impression of a much older man—a contemporary of James, she had decided in her own mind. For an endless moment, she made herself look down at the table, trying to pretend she was oblivious to his regard.

'Is your name Christow?' She had not heard his approach and she started violently, spilling a little of her drink. His voice was low and resonant, but held no welcoming warmth.

Gabrielle looked up reluctantly. He was standing over her, his thumb hooked negligently into his belt. At close quarters, the attraction she had only sensed across the room was quite devastating and she was conscious that they were the cynosure of envious feminine eyes from adjoining tables.

'Yes,' she said at last, 'I'm Gabrielle Christow. And you?'

His face was narrow, the cheekbones and jawline prominent, with dark hair in need of cutting springing aggressively back from his forehead. Against his deep tan, his eyes were as pale as aquamarines. They held incredulity and hostility in almost equal amounts.

He said slowly, 'My God, I don't believe it. The fools! The bloody, incompetent fools!'

Gabrielle stiffened, aware as he was not of the interested ears surrounding them.

She said with a hint of ice, 'I'm afraid I don't follow you.'

'No?' One of the slanting dark eyebrows lifted in a sardonic question. 'Were you naïvely expecting to be welcomed with open arms? If so, I'm afraid, young woman, you're in for a sharp disappointment.'

Gabrielle was very pale. She stammered, 'But I thought

—I mean, *Vision* made all the arrangements—I understood I was expected.'

'We were expecting a photographer from *Vision* to join us—yes.'

There was no doubting the implication in his words and she glared at him.

'Are you questioning my professional competence?' she demanded hotly.

'That's the least of my concerns.' He hitched forward a chair, and straddled the seat, his arms folded across the back of the chair. 'In any case, I shall not be in a position to judge it.'

'Meaning?'

'Meaning that you'll be on the next flight back to Europe from Mexico City as soon as it can be arranged. We'll cable *Vision* and if they care to do a hasty re-think and send us a replacement before we leave, all well and good. If not . . .' He shrugged.

'A replacement?' she echoed dazedly. 'But why?'

'I should have thought it would have been obvious even to the meanest intelligence.' The cool blue eyes went over her from the chic sandals to the scooped neckline of the sleeveless white dress. 'This assignment is not for a woman, Miss Christow.'

For a stunned moment she looked at him, then she managed a brief, scornful laugh. 'What kind of absurd prejudice is this, may I ask?'

'Ask away.' He produced a cheroot from a case and lit it. 'It has nothing to do with prejudice—just ordinary common sense. The rain forest is no place for an inexperienced girl. I should have thought your editor would have had more sense.'

Gabrielle shook her head in disbelief. It had been bad enough coming from James, but to come all this way and get the same reception from a complete stranger was almost more than she could bear.

She said coldly, 'In Britain now women have equal opportunities with men. Legally we can no longer be discriminated against on the grounds of sex.'

'That's fine for Britain.' He drew deeply on the cheroot. 'But it cuts no ice in the Yucatan—which is where you are, in case you hadn't noticed. The expedition we're involved in has dangers and discomforts you've never even imagined in your comfortable London office. A man could—just—have made it. But you?' He spread his hands, his eyes going over her dismissively. 'No way.'

Gabrielle stood up angrily, ignoring the speculative looks being directed at them from all over the foyer.

'I should prefer to continue this—discussion somewhere less public,' she said in a low voice.

'Willingly.' His smile lifted the corners of his firm-lipped mouth. 'My place or yours?'

Gabrielle felt her cheeks redden in spite of herself.

'Professor Morgan . . .' she began in angry protest.

He shook his head. 'Wrong again, I'm afraid. My name is Lennox—Shaun Lennox. Dennis Morgan is ill—a touch of fever.'

She stared at him, a glimmer of hope appearing on her bleak horizon. 'You mean you're not even the leader of the expedition and yet you presume to come here—to give me my marching orders as if . . .'

'Yes, I do so presume.' His brows snapped together. No laughter now. 'Dennis is not a young man any more and he's been quite sick. I want to spare him as many minor worries and irritations as possible.'

Gabrielle lifted her chin. 'I suppose there's no need to ask which classification I come under. Well, I don't want to cause Professor Morgan any anxiety either, and I'm quite prepared to wait until he's well again for his decision.'

'I can assure you it will be the same as mine.'

'Perhaps.' Gabrielle suddenly felt as if she gained the advantage and pressed it home eagerly. 'But I'd prefer to hear it from his own lips—if you don't mind,' she added sweetly.

'Please yourself,' he said shortly. 'I suppose, having come all this way, you're entitled to a few days' holiday at *Vision*'s expense. They probably owe it to you, anyway, having sent you here under false pretences.'

'We'll see about that,' Gabrielle asserted confidently. Then a new and disturbing thought occurred to her. 'Er—about my accommodation.'

He leaned forward and stubbed out his cheroot in an ash tray. 'What about it?'

She flushed. 'Well, I'm booked in here for tonight, but I understood—that is, Martin said that I would be staying at the Institute headquarters—as part of the team.'

She did not add that this assumption had also been based on the fact that she was married to a member of the team as well.

'An excellent idea—if you'd been the accredited representative we were expecting. As things are, maybe you'd do better to stay here.'

She looked at him, frankly dismayed. 'But they may not have a vacancy. This is the tourist season, you know.'

'Yes,' he said gently, 'I know.'

His eyes were completely impassive as they met the indignation in hers. Gabrielle controlled herself with an effort and marched over to the reception desk. But the clerk met her halting inquiry with a blank face and a regretful shake of the head. There were no reservations available after that night. The hotel was full and he was unable to recommend anywhere else which might have a vacancy. Merida, he explained with much hand-waving, was full for the season—except for certain places where the *señorita* would not care to stay.

'I shouldn't be too sure,' Gabrielle commented under her breath.

She walked back to the table, fighting an impulse to

throw herself on this Lennox man's dubious mercy and beg a lodging at the Institute. At the same time, she was deeply concerned by the reaction her arrival had caused. Was it possible that James had kept to himself the fact that the *Vision* photographer Professor Morgan was expecting was his wife? Was he dissociating himself from her completely. It was a troubling thought and made her position in Merida even more tenuous.

As she approached the table, she saw that Shaun Lennox had risen and was waiting for her, his hands resting lightly on his hips, a faint smile playing about his mouth. It was the smile that decided her. She would sleep in the street rather than ask any favour of him.

She forced an answering smile. 'That's settled,' she said with spurious brightness. She hesitated. 'Would it be in order for me to at least *visit* the Institute?' She indicated the big square case on the floor. 'Some of my cameras and equipment are valuable, and I'd feel happier if I could get them under lock and key there, rather than leave them in my room.'

He eyed the case expressionlessly. 'I suppose that can be arranged,' he said drily. 'But don't regard it as a foot in the door.'

She breathed a silent sigh of relief. She was sure she could find somewhere to stay if she no longer had her cameras to worry about. She had brought the minimum of luggage with her, feeling it was better to make up any deficiencies locally if necessary.

Besides, it was only too likely that the first person she came face to face with at the Institute would be James himself, and then her accommodation problem would surely be solved. Even James, she thought, could hardly repudiate his own wife in front of his colleagues without causing the sort of unpleasant scene that he would detest. She noted with a feeling of resignation that she seemed to have abandoned the idea of any kind of welcome from James.

'Well, let's go.' Shaun Lennox's voice broke impatiently across the depressing trend of her thoughts. 'I've wasted enough time today already. That case is all you need to take, I assume. You'll need your other luggage with you.'

Gabrielle, who had been searching for an excuse to take her large suitcase along as well, let the idea drop with an inward sigh. She could always, she supposed, tell this forbidding stranger her real identity and have the joy of seeing him eat humble pie over his rudeness to a colleague's wife, but she was reluctant to do so. It would involve her in all kinds of awkward explanations at this late stage and if these were needed she would prefer to make them to Professor Morgan. But she hoped at the same time that they would not be necessary. James could not just go on ignoring the fact of her presence for ever.

'Of course,' she said, disliking him more than she would ever have thought possible.

'Right, then.' He glanced rather ostentatiously at his watch and she bent to pick up the heavy case, shifting her shoulder bag to the other side as she did so. It was an awkward movement, rendered even more so by the fact that she caught her sandal heel against the leg of the table and overbalanced, stumbling slightly.

'So your much vaunted sexual equality doesn't extend to carrying your own baggage,' he commented drily, and before she could protest, he had swung the case to his own shoulder. 'Can you manage now, Miss Christow?'

She glared at him impotently. 'Thank you—yes.'

But once outside the hotel where a jeep stood waiting, another hazard presented itself. Although the rain had stopped almost as suddenly as it had begun, the street was still more like a miniature river than a highway and Gabrielle halted on the hotel steps with an exclamation of dismay.

'Come now, Miss Christow. Didn't anyone ever tell you that Merida is also known as Little Venice—among other things?' he added with a sardonic curl of his lips.

'No, they didn't, Mr Lennox.' She kept her voice cool. 'That's why I'm wearing sandals—not waders.'

Again she had to endure that look of total assessment that seemed to reach her shrinking skin.

'I'm sure your job requires that you get your facts straight,' he drawled. 'It's Dr Lennox, not Mr. And there's no need to paddle, as long as you're prepared to forgo your liberated woman's principles yet again.'

He placed her camera case in the back of the jeep and before she could speak or move, reached for her in turn. He lifted her as easily as if she had been a doll, her legs dangling helplessly as she was held for an endless, unbearable moment against his hard muscular body, then with almost insolent ease he deposited her none too gently in the passenger seat. Gabrielle sat up, straightening her dress and smoothing her hair with hands that shook in spite of her efforts to control them, while he strode round to the other side of the jeep and swung himself into the driving seat.

He grinned at her, as he switched on the ignition.

'We get more than our feet wet in the rain forest, Miss Christow,' he said laconically. 'Count yourself lucky to be out of it.'

'We'll see about that, Dr Lennox.' Her tone held a restrained fury that could not have been lost on him. A moment's pause and she added, 'Male chauvinist pig isn't a phrase I ever thought I would use, but in your case I have to make an exception.'

'Well, don't feel badly about it, Miss Christow.' The jeep set off with a perceptible jerk and Gabrielle realised that her jibe had actually got to him. 'There's bound to be a female equivalent and I should have no hesitation in using it about you—if you're around that long.'

And there was no answer to that, Gabrielle thought with a sinking heart.

CHAPTER TWO

It was a relatively short drive to the Institute headquarters, but it seemed longer to Gabrielle. The silence between them seemed to crackle, but neither she nor her companion made the slightest attempt to relieve the tension by introducing some casual topic of conversation.

There was plenty she would have liked to have asked him, especially when she caught a glimpse down a side street of the huge pale lemon mass of the sixteenth-century cathedral. It was infuriating to think she had been kicking her heels in the hotel waiting for the Institute to contact her, and now that she did have a chance to do some sight-seeing, it was being spoiled for her like this.

It was hard to maintain her reserve when they swung into a wide, busy boulevard lined on each side by big houses, most of which had the unmistakable appearance of having seen better days, and built in a crazy jumble of varying architectural styles. Gabrielle's hands itched for her camera. She found all this forlorn grandeur intensely appealing, but the jeep sped on and she had to be content with promising herself a return visit on her own before she left Merida.

They turned off presently into a narrower thoroughfare, where the exotic topiary hedges gave way to high white walls, interspersed with anonymous wooden gates, and it was outside one of these that the jeep eventually drew up. The drainage must be better in some parts of the city than others, Gabrielle thought, as she noticed that the narrow pavement on which she was about to descend seemed to have escaped the recent flooding.

Dr Lennox had already reached into the back of the jeep

and recovered her camera case. Now he stood unsmilingly, holding it while he extended his other hand to help her out of the jeep. Perversely, she ignored his proffered assistance and climbed down unaided, uncomfortably aware as she did so that the manoeuvre had revealed more of her slim legs than she had intended. But if she had expected some pointed comment, none was forthcoming. He merely unlatched the gate and stood aside to allow her to precede him.

The courtyard they entered was surrounded on three sides by an attractive two-storey building in white stucco. A covered verandah ran the length of the ground floor and was echoed by a series of connecting balconies on the upper floor. A fountain played lazily in the centre of the tiled yard and brilliant blossoms flowered in tubs or swarmed in heady splendour over the columns of the verandah.

Gabrielle drew an appreciative breath, but her companion seemed oblivious to the charm of their surroundings and showed no disposition to linger. He strode across the yard and up the steps to a pair of imposing louvred doors set in the middle of the verandah facing them. Gabrielle followed him, aware of a sudden pounding in her chest, and damp palms which owed nothing to the prevailing humidity.

She found herself in a large entrance hall, looking across the exquisitely blocked parquet floor to where a graceful staircase with a wrought iron balustrade swept up in a leisurely curve to the floor above. There were several doors in the hall, all forbiddingly shut, but from behind one of them came the sound of typewriters. Dr Lennox walked to this door and threw it open with an impatient twist of the elaborate handle.

It was a large room, giving an impression of space in spite of the efficient desks, filing cabinets and small switchboard it contained.

Two girls were busy typing while a third seemed occupied with a mass of official-looking forms, but she looked up with a smile at the newcomers, her gaze lingering questioningly on Gabrielle.

'*Esta es la* Señorita Christow,' Dr Lennox remarked, apparently to the room at large. He indicated the camera case he was carrying. 'Isabella, could you find a safe place for this, *por favor*?'

'*Si.*' The girl rose, quietly composed in her dark dress, her black hair neatly confined at the nape of her neck. 'Perhaps I should put it in the strong-room.'

Her voice rose questioningly and Dr Lennox turned to Gabrielle. 'Does that satisfy?' His voice was chilly.

'Thank you.' Gabrielle moistened her lips and smiled over-brightly at Isabella. '*Gracias*. That will be fine. You're very kind.'

'*No hay de que. De nada.*' Isabella lifted her shoulders in a graceful shrug. She paused. 'You—are going to work here, *señorita*?'

'I hope so,' Gabrielle said awkwardly, acutely aware of the tall man who lounged beside her in the doorway, listening.

'Don't they say "Hope springs eternal in the human breast"?' he interjected drily before Isabella could begin the polite reply which was already forming on her lips. 'My advice to you, Miss Christow, is to book your return flight and save yourself and everyone else a lot of needless argument and trouble.'

'That might be more convenient from your point of view, Dr Lennox, but I am here to work, not to creep home with my tail between my legs because of some whim of yours. I prefer to wait for Professor Morgan's decision!'

'As you wish.' He shrugged negligently. 'Now, if you'll excuse me, I have work to do. Isabella will arrange for Carlos to drive you back to your hotel. Unless common sense prevails with you in the meantime, I expect we shall be in touch. *Hasta luego*, Miss Christow.'

Gabrielle felt curiously solitary as the tall figure vanished. She turned back to Isabella, but the girl was already busy at the switchboard, presumably summoning the unknown Carlos. She was to be summarily hustled off the premises, it seemed.

She gave the other girl a perfunctory smile and wandered back into the hall. The building was very quiet suddenly. Even the distant traffic sounded no louder than the drowsy hum of bees. It was a surprisingly tranquil place, she thought. Too tranquil for someone as abrasive as Dr Lennox. She stared round restlessly at the quiet elegance of the hall, and her attention sharpened as she realised that some of the tall carved doors bore neat name-plates. Could they be the private offices of some of the Institute employees? If so, one of them could be James'. He might be working in there now, totally unaware of her presence. Her fingers clenched a little as she registered the bareness of her left hand. While things remained as they were between them, she had decided not to wear her wedding ring. It was in her small jewellery box at the bottom of her suitcase and it would stay there until matters were resolved.

'You want something, *señorita*?' Isabella was standing in the office doorway watching her. She was smiling no longer, and her piquant face held a faintly suspicious look.

'It's all right,' Gabrielle said quickly. 'I'm just—absorbing the atmosphere. It's such a lovely building, isn't it?'

Isabella shrugged, a little dismissively. '*Es muy viejo*—very old,' she enlarged unwillingly, but she did not offer to show Gabrielle around any of it as she had half hoped she might. In fact, her earlier friendliness had evaporated—with the departure of Dr Lennox, Gabrielle realised ironically.

She badly wanted to read the names on some of those doors—but not while she was being watched. She glanced around, improvising rapidly. 'It's very hot, isn't it? *Muy caliente*. I wonder if I could have a drink?'

Isabella frowned slightly. 'There will be fruit juice. You want that I fetch?'

'If you would be so kind.' Gabrielle made herself smile winningly at her.

Isabella muttered something unintelligible in Spanish, then with an ungracious, 'Be good enough to wait here, *señorita*,' she disappeared down the hall. Gabrielle waited until the click of her heels had died into silence, then whipped across and began examining the nameplates. She had worked down one side of the hall and was just beginning on the other, her ears straining to catch the sound of Isabella's return, when she found what she was looking for. 'Dr. J. A. Warner', the card stated. For a moment she hesitated, then lifted her hand determinedly and knocked. When there was no reply, she knocked again more loudly, then turned the carved handle and went in.

The anti-climax was complete. The room was quite empty. But it was not merely James' physical presence that was lacking, Gabrielle realised as she glanced round. Both desk and filing cabinet seemed oddly bare—no comfortable clutter of papers or maps—no pen thrown down as if the room's occupant would soon be back to resume his interrupted work. The waste basket was empty, and the bookshelves looked as if their contents had been severely pruned. There were a few standard works which Gabrielle recognised as also occupying a place in James' study at home and a sprinkling of rather dog-eared pamphlets. Gabrielle felt oddly disturbed. At home, James had stamped his personality on the flat—obsessively so. Here, he seemed to have made no impression at all. There was no trace of him—not even an empty pipe.

Engrossed in her thoughts, her first consciousness that she was no longer alone came with Isabella's shrill '*Que hace usted aqui*? What are you doing here, *señorita*?' from behind her.

Gabrielle turned hastily and saw the other girl standing

in the doorway, holding a glass of fruit juice.

'I'm sorry,' she apologised quickly. 'I—I wanted somewhere to sit down and there were no seats in the hall.'

'*Es privado*. Entrance is not permitted to these rooms—there are items of value. If you wish to sit, there is a bench in the courtyard.'

Gabrielle stiffened. Was Isabella insinuating that she looked like a thief? But she controlled her temper with an effort. After all, her conduct was questionable and Isabella was justified at least in judging her a snooper. It would have been far better to have introduced herself properly and asked for James quite openly, she thought unhappily, but having embarked on this course, she would have to continue with it. She had no intention of explaining herself to Isabella.

She made her voice equable. 'I didn't know these rooms were private or I wouldn't have intruded. But I don't see any valuable items—in fact the place looks deserted. Does—does anyone use it?'

'*Si*, Dr Warner uses it.'

'Do you know where he is?' Gabrielle found she was holding her breath.

Isabella stared at her. 'Why should I know? It is not my concern. There is much work now because soon an expedition starts to the Chiapas. Maybe Dr Warner is in Villahermosa making arrangements. Who knows?'

'In Villahermosa? Are you sure?'

Isabella gave her a look of baffled hostility. 'I am sure of nothing, *señorita*, but it is certain that he *was* there—with Dr Lennox. Maybe he stays there.'

Gabrielle could have groaned aloud, but she had already given Isabella too much fuel for her curiosity, she realised.

She said, hating the inanity in her voice, 'Oh—of course. They'll all be so busy. I didn't think ... Is that juice for me? How lovely. I think I will sit down—in the courtyard, did you say?'

Isabella's eyes were openly contemptuous now. 'Carlos is waiting for you, *señorita.* He too has other work to attend to,' she mentioned abruptly. She turned and waited ostentatiously for Gabrielle to precede her into the hall. Then she closed James' door with rather more than necessary force before marching across the hall to her own office without a backward glance.

'And *hasta la vista* to you too,' Gabrielle thought wryly as she sipped her drink. She wandered out into the sunshine and stood listening to the splash of the fountain as she finished the contents of the glass. She left the empty glass on the bench as she turned to greet Carlos who came out of the Institute to meet her. He was small and round with a warm smile, and he looked oddly familiar, although she was hard put to it to discover where the familiarity lay. It wasn't until they were in the jeep and driving away and she saw him in profile that she knew. It was the typically Mayan profile that she had seen in endless pictures and reproductions, even to the slightly sloping forehead. It made the jungle palaces seem suddenly far less remote.

The return drive to the hotel was an altogether different proposition. Carlos needed no urging to deviate from the direct route and show off his abilities as a guide.

'But a jeep is not the best way to see Merida, *señorita,*' he told her reproachfully. 'Tomorrow you must walk to the Plaza de la Indepencia and see the Casa Montejo.'

'Wasn't it a Montejo who founded Merida?' Gabrielle searched her memory for the facts she had assimilated during her background reading on the Yucatan.

'*Si.* Don Francisco de Montejo. He conquered forty thousand Indians with only four hundred Spanish knights. Our beautiful cathedral is built on the spot where he won his victory.'

Gabrielle sighed a little. 'Quite a victory,' she said drily. 'And all in the name of God, I suppose.'

'Si, *señorita.* How could it be otherwise? And in the

cathedral, there is a beautiful picture of the visit of the king Tutul XIV visiting Don Francisco only weeks before his conversion to our blessed faith.'

Whatever the physical evidence might be, Carlos had chosen his own ancestors, Gabrielle realised, hiding a smile.

'I think your Mexico is very beautiful, Carlos,' she said.

Carlos gave her a disgusted look. 'Is not *my* Mexico, *señorita.* I was born a Yucateco. I do not concern myself with Mexico.' He removed his hands from the wheel to snap his fingers as a sign of his sublime disregard for both Mexico and the mass of traffic around them.

Gabrielle was sorely tempted to laugh, but managed to retain her self-control. 'I'm sorry, Carlos. I didn't realise feeling was so strong here.'

He grinned cheerfully. 'We belong to ourselves, *señorita,* that is all. For so long we were alone that we became—accustomed.'

It was probably true, Gabrielle thought, visualising the small Spanish outpost that the *conquistadores* had set up on the peninsula and held against all odds.

Carlos was continuing, pointing out places of interest as they passed and recommending restaurants. 'And when you are too tired to walk any further, *señorita,* you can go to the Parque Cepada and take a *calesa* for the rest of your tour.'

Gabrielle nodded a smiling agreement. She had already promised herself a ride in one of the pony-drawn buggies which could be seen everywhere on the streets. But before she embarked on any of these pleasures, she silently reminded herself, she had to find somewhere to stay. She nearly asked Carlos if he could help her, but bit the words back at the last moment. She had led that Lennox man to believe that she could continue to stay at her hotel. She did not want him to find out the truth through some chance remark from Carlos.

She was half toying with the idea of hiring a car to take her to Villahermosa, but common sense intervened. At least in Merida she had a contact—however tenuous—with the Institute. Sooner or later, James would return there. If she went to Villahermosa she would be searching for a needle in a haystack, and there was every chance that she would miss him again.

She ate a solitary dinner in the hotel dining room, very conscious that she seemed to be the only person in the room on her own. She ordered *enchilada*, but asked for it to be accompanied by a tomato sauce instead of the usual red chilli accompaniment until her palate had adjusted to the new highly spiced dishes. The last thing she wanted was a touch of 'Montezuma's Revenge', especially if she was homeless, she thought wryly.

She was drinking the last of a reflective cup of coffee when she heard someone speak to her, and glancing up, she saw a couple, not many years older than herself, who had been sitting at the next table. They introduced themselves as Jon and Cathy Benson and needed no urging to accept Gabrielle's rather tentative invitation to join her for more coffee. They seemed a friendly, outgoing pair and she soon learned that they were from California and were enjoying a delayed 'honeymoon' after five years of marriage. They obviously believed she was yet another eager tourist like themselves, and they were wide-eyed with interest as Gabrielle explained the work she hoped to do.

'Gee, you're lucky,' Cathy sighed. 'We have to start for home next week. Have you visited many of the sites yet? We stopped over to see Bonampak and Palenque on the way here. Oh boy, the Temple of the Inscriptions—it's just so—tremendous. I felt like some kind of ant.'

Her husband laughed. 'Cath's exaggerating as usual,' he teased. 'Not even a Mayan temple could put her down.'

'Oh no?' Cathy laid her hand over her heart with an extravagant gesture. 'Reading about all those human sacrifices gave me some genuinely bad moments, I can tell you.'

Gabrielle smiled. 'I expect they had roughly the same effect on the victims,' she said drily.

Jon shuddered. 'This is a great after-dinner conversation! What we really came across to say was that a group of us are going to La Ermita tonight and as you seem to be alone, we wondered if you would care to come along too.'

'La Ermita?' Gabrielle looked at them questioningly. 'What—or where—is that?'

'It's an old hermitage on the outskirts. It's been restored and they've made a garden out of the old cemetery next door. At night, it's all lit up and there's even a waterfall. They have music and there are usually dancers that you can watch.' Cathy laid an eager hand on her arm. 'Come with us and see for yourself. We love it there.'

Gabrielle was sorely tempted. Things had gone so badly for her, it seemed, ever since she had first set foot in the Yucatan that the idea of an evening of gaiety appealed to her strongly. But at the same time, she was reluctant to leave the hotel in case James tried to contact her, although that was beginning to seem an increasingly remote possibility. And she also had the prospect of a strenuous day ahead of her, searching for fresh accommodation, she remembered.

She was genuinely regretful as she refused the invitation, and was warmed by the Bensons' disappointment at her refusal, as well as their cheerful assurances that they wouldn't take no for an answer next time. It was the first friendly reaction she'd had from anyone since she arrived in Mexico, she thought as she left the dining room, and instantly choked down the lump that rose in her throat at the thought. Self-pity was one of the last emotions she could afford to waste her energies on, she told herself resolutely as she went up to her room. She showered and climbed into bed, reaching for the book that stood on her bedside table. It was a modern account of the re-discovery of the Maya by Stephens and Catherwood during the 1840s, and reminding herself of the trials and sufferings they had endured in the rain forest would, she hoped, help her to get her own problems in perspective. But when, eventually, she fell into a troubled sleep, dreaming confusedly of jungle courts and creeper-hung palaces, it was not the pale bearded face of any Victorian explorer which stared at her from the shadowed doorways and arches but the dark, arrogant face of Shaun Lennox.

Gabrielle shifted her suitcase from one hand to another yet again, pausing to flex the muscles in her aching arm. She had stayed around the Hotel Belen as long as possible, hoping for the reprieve of a last-minute cancellation, but none had been forthcoming and she had realised eventually that she would have to vacate her room.

She had been on the point of departure when she had encountered the Bensons and she had felt foolishly embarrassed, as if she was leaving the hotel under some kind of cloud. They were naturally surprised to see her carrying her suitcase, but they accepted her rather halting explanation that she was transferring to the Institute without too much demur. She knew that if she had given one hint of her predicament, they would probably have offered to drive her round Merida until she found somewhere to stay, but at the same time she felt it would be unfair to involve them in her troubles when their own holiday was drawing to an end and they would want to make the most of the time they had left in the Yucatan.

Now she wished she had not been quite so altruistic. She might have found explanations slightly humiliating, but not as bad as this utterly fruitless trek from hotel to lodging house that had occupied most of the day. She had used a local guide book to draw up a list of the more likely places to try, but this was almost exhausted now and it was nearing sunset. She had to find somewhere quickly, she thought with alarm. It would be unthinkable to be out on the streets with her case after dark.

The Bensons had promised cheerfully to 'Keep in touch' as they said goodbye, and Gabrielle found herself longing for them to appear by magic in their big blue car and take charge. But that was negative thinking, she chided herself mentally. It was tantamount to admitting that Shaun Lennox could be right, and that she was out of her depth here.

She stifled a quick sigh and took a firm grip of her suitcase. She had one more place in her list—the Café Tula, which offered a few rooms to rent above its ground floor premises. She crossed her fingers superstitiously, hoping rather desperately that they might still have a vacant corner somewhere they could offer her.

Her spirits rose a little as she went in and glanced round at the neat booths with their solid-looking tables and benches and the spotlessly clean tablecloths. Several of the booths were already occupied by diners and an invitingly spicy smell of cooking drifted in from the kitchen. There was a well-stocked bar at one end of the room and a man was standing behind it arranging bottles on a shelf. He turned as Gabrielle approached rather diffidently.

'*Quisiera una habitacion, por favor,*' she asked politely. the Spanish phrase requesting a room rising almost fluently to her lips after a day of practice.

The man studied her for a moment without reply. He had a round placid face with a slightly anxious expression. Then with a slight shrug, he called 'Pilar!' and turned back to his task.

Almost at once, the swing doors to the kitchen bounced open and a small, dark woman swathed in a white apron swept into the room. She paused, her hands resting aggressively on her hips. The swift flood of Spanish, directed primarily at the man behind the counter, was too fast for Gabrielle to follow, but from the tone and the accompanying gestures she gathered that Pilar was far from pleased at being brought from her stove to deal with a passing *turista.*

'Que quiere usted, señorita?' Her voice was brusque and impatient and Gabrielle flushed a little, and repeated her request for a room.

'No hay ningunas?' The woman spoke dismissively and turned as if to go back to the kitchen.

'Oh, wait—please.' Gabrielle spoke in English in her alarm. *'Señora, estoy cansada.* I'm tired—I need a room. *Es urgente,'* she added on a note of appeal.

But the only response from Pilar was a sniff, followed by another tirade in Spanish, none of which was comprehensible to Gabrielle. The man behind the bar tried to intervene but was silenced with a look. Gabrielle turned towards him impulsively.

'Señor, I don't understand what your wife is saying. Can you explain to her that I'm not a tourist? I am—working here in Merida for a while. I do need a room very badly and I'm willing to pay whatever she asks.'

As she spoke, Gabrielle fumbled in her bag for her wallet, but the man shook his head.

'Is not—money, *señorita.* Is—no room,' he said haltingly, but he looked uncomfortable and his eyes did not meet Gabrielle's as he spoke.

Pilar muttered something to him, then swung away and returned to her kitchen. The man sighed.

'My wife says Hernandez may have room. The *señorita* should try there.'

'Hernandez?' Gabrielle was puzzled. It was not one of the names on her list nor one she had encountered in any of the guides, but it seemed she had little choice other than to go along with the suggestion. She produced a scrap of paper and a pen from her bag and laid it on the bar counter. *'Como puedo ir a Hernandez, señor, por favor?'*

With another sigh, he drew her a brief sketch map, then

turned away with an air of relief to serve some customers who had just arrived.

So much for the famed hospitality of the Yucatan, Gabrielle thought with an inward grimace as she hoisted her case and prepared to set off on her travels again.

Her uncertainty increased when she finally arrived at the place indicated on the map. It was not the small restaurant or *posada* she had envisaged but a small bar in a side street, its sign picked out in gaudy electric bulbs, many of which were either broken or missing. A beaded curtain gave access to the bar from the street and after a momentary hesitation, she pushed this aside and entered. Her nose wrinkled involuntarily as she glanced around. It had none of the clean, comfortable atmosphere of the Café Tula. The interior lighting was poor and a few noisy fans fixed to the walls were the nearest approach to air conditioning. The customers appeared to be all men and Gabrielle paused, fighting an instinctive urge to turn and go back to the dark street outside. Anywhere—even a bench in one of the plazas—would be better than this, she thought despairingly, before common sense came to rescue her, reminding her not to judge by appearances alone and that she had, anyway, very little choice in the matter.

'*Si, señorita*? Can I help you?' A large man who had been sitting alone at a corner table reading a newspaper heaved himself to his feet and came forward, his eyes roaming over her. He was an unprepossessing individual, his dirty shirt straining the buttons over his belly, while his smile revealed broken and discoloured teeth. But his voice was polite enough and Gabrielle forced herself to return his smile.

With the feeling she was living through some kind of bad dream, she explained her predicament in her halting Spanish and saw his smile broaden.

'*No norteamericana*?' he asked.

Gabrielle shook her head. '*Inglesa*,' she returned.

'And who tells an *Inglesa* to come to Hernandez?'

'They sent me from the Café Tula. A woman called Pilar told me to try here.' Gabrielle was relieved that his command of English seemed so good.

'Pilar told you, eh?' He was overcome by a spasm of silent laughter, his shoulders heaving up and down appreciatively. 'It—figures. Pilar does not like *gringas*.' He reached down and picked up Gabrielle's case. 'I show you the room, *señorita*.'

Gabrielle followed him across the room, embarrassedly aware of the frankly assessing glances fixed on her from all sides. She found herself uneasily checking that all the buttons on her navy shirt were fastened and that the cream flare of her skirt hadn't been caught up in any way. She was almost glad to find herself out of the bar and going up a narrow stairway between stained and peeling walls. She felt a shiver of distaste which she firmly quelled. Whatever the room was like, she could put up with it for one night at least. Tomorrow she could make fresh plans—maybe even go to Villahermosa.

But the room was not as bad as she had anticipated. The floor was uncarpeted, and some of the slats were broken in the shutters at the windows, but the brightly patterned bedcover seemed clean and so did the cracked washbasin in the corner.

She turned to Hernandez. 'How much is the room, *señor*?'

The price he named made her gasp in disbelief. 'I—I couldn't possibly afford all that!'

He shrugged. 'But the *señorita* is working. It is a fair rent.'

Now how did he know that? she wondered helplessly. She tried to speak firmly.

'I am—hoping to work, yes, but nothing is settled yet, and I haven't a great deal of money. Besides, I only want the room for one night,' she added hastily.

Hernandez' large greasy face creased into a frown. '*Que?* But the *señorita* is *muy hermosa.* She will not take long to find—work. But I am not a hard man. I make a reduction now and later we talk again.'

Gabrielle accepted with relief, deciding it might be better not to continue any argument about the length of her proposed stay. She handed over the money and watched Hernandez count it before stowing it away in his pocket. He gave her another ingratiating smile as he prepared to leave. 'The *señorita* want anything? Tequila?'

'Thank you, no.' Gabrielle said hastily. Her empty stomach revolted at the thought of alcohol. She would have to find a restaurant nearby and have something to eat, she thought, flinching a little from the prospect of having to face another trip through the bar downstairs, and wishing that she'd had the foresight to buy some food during the day.

She was glad to see the back of Hernandez, who had seemed disposed to linger, but her heart sank when she finally closed the door behind him and discovered there was no lock on it, and a small broken bolt. She groaned aloud. If she did go out, what guarantee did she have that any of her belongings would still be here when she returned? She gazed rather desperately round the room, registering the fact that the door of the small wardrobe had to be wedged shut with newspaper. It looked as if she was a prisoner in her room until morning. Wearily she picked up her case and put it on the bed. She might as well try and get some sleep and forget her hunger that way.

She found her nightdress and slippers and closed the case again. There was no point in unpacking any further when she would be out of here first thing in the morning, she thought. She swung the case off the bed and looked round for somewhere to stow it. Under the bed seemed the most obvious place and she lifted a corner of the bedcover to make sure there was room.

Something—more than one—ran. Black, bloated and shining from the sheltering darkness under the bed, almost brushing her hand in passing. Her skin crawled uncontrollably and she heard herself scream in pure panic. She jumped to her feet, pulling the covers back from the bed with shaking hands, determined to find if there were any more lurking horrors.

'What is the matter? Why are you shouting?' Hernandez was back again. His voice sounded irritable through the closed door. She threw it open and confronted him.

'There are cockroaches in this room, *señor*!'

He looked at her almost incredulously and gave a short laugh. 'So? Perhaps you should have taken a room at the Montejo Palace, *gringa*.'

She bit her lip. 'I'll need some insecticide. And a bucket of water, some disinfectant and a mop. I'm going to clean this room.'

Hernandez came in and shut the door behind him. He smiled at her genially, but Gabrielle felt a quiver of alarm run along her nerve endings.

'Why do you make so much fuss? The room is cheap, no, and the—clients when they come do not notice such things. The other girls do not complain.'

Dry-throated, Gabrielle said, 'Other girls?'

'*Si*. You do not imagine you are the first? But you were wise to come to Hernandez, *Inglesa*. I will—look after you.'

The expression in his eyes as he watched her made her feel as if she was swimming through slime. Trying to keep her voice steady, she said, 'I think there has been some mistake. I'd better leave.'

His small eyes narrowed. 'Why you go? Soon everyone will know there is an *Inglesa* at Hernandez' place. Many will come. You will make a lot of money. You were a fool to go to Pilar. Pilar is a good woman—very moral—go to Mass each day.'

'No,' she said desperately. 'You don't understand . . .'

'I understand.' He shrugged negligently. 'You had to leave your hotel. Hotels here—very strict. But is O.K. here. Is good room, very cheap.' He smiled again and took her arm, pinching the flesh between his stubby fingers. 'Be nice to Hernandez, *gringa*, and maybe the room gets cheaper.'

Sheer panic lent her extra strength. She tore herself free from his grip and dodged past him out of the room, intent only on reaching the street and the comparative safety it seemed to offer. But there was a man coming up the dark stairs, blocking them. She collided with a hard body. Arms like steel bands went round her, controlling her struggles, as sobs of fright tore at her throat.

'Calm down!' The voice held a snarl, but it was English and it was also familiar. Dazedly, Gabrielle looked up into Shaun Lennox's dark face, his eyes brilliant with anger.

'What are you doing here?' she gasped.

'I could ask you the same, but it's hardly the time for damfool questions.' He took her arm in a bruising grip and led her back down the passage, ignoring her instinctive resistance. 'Don't abandon your luggage, Miss Christow. Hernandez will only sell it, and I imagine he's had some money from you already. Don't let him make more profit from your mistake.'

Hernandez was standing sulkily by the door as they went in. At the sight of Shaun Lennox, his whole attitude became defensive and he embarked on what seemed to be lengthy explanations in Spanish, causing every now and then to shoot accusing glares at Gabrielle.

Dr Lennox silenced him with one swift phrase which brought dull colour into the swarthy cheeks. Then he turned to Gabrielle.

'Get your things together, Miss Christow,' he advised curtly. 'They're holding dinner for us at the Institute.'

She stared at him unbelievingly for a moment. 'What made you change your mind?'

'I haven't,' he said succinctly. 'Dennis Morgan has made one of his lightning recoveries and wants to have a look at you. I phoned your hotel this morning to let you know and found you'd left without a forwarding address. We've been looking for you most of the day.'

'How did you find me?' She rolled her nightdress into a ball and rammed it into a corner of the case.

'Quite by accident. Rosita who works in the office at the Institute—you may have seen her yesterday—was dining at the Café Tula with her *novio* tonight and she saw you. She got the gist of what was going on and it worried her, especially when she heard friend Hernandez' name being mentioned. This bar is pretty notorious. But her English isn't too good and she doubted whether she'd be able to make you understand, so she telephoned me instead.'

'I'm very gateful to her.' Gabrielle snapped the locks on her case with trembling fingers.

'You have good reason to be,' he said drily. 'From your dramatic appearance just now, I imagine I came just in time. Here.' He held out an imperative hand for the case and she surrendered it without a word.

The jeep was parked outside. She climbed in, still without speaking and sat, staring rigidly ahead through the windscreen. Shaun Lennox joined her.

'I think I'm going to be sick,' she said in a tight little voice.

'You're just hungry.' He started the engine. 'Try and think about something else.'

'How can I think of anything else?' There was an edge of hysteria in her voice. 'You don't know the sort of day I've been through. And now this!'

'You were warned,' he reminded her. 'I told you that this was not the place for practising your new-found sexual equality or women's liberation—or any other half-baked ideas for that matter. But you had to find out the hard way.

Why didn't you tell me the Belen wanted your room and that you were stranded?'

'You know why!' she flashed.

'Pride, I suppose.' His lips twisted wryly. 'And if Rosita hadn't recognised you just now—I wonder how much pride you'd have had left in the morning. Would you have thought it was worth it?'

The tears which had been threatening forced their way to the surface and spilled over. She felt totally humiliated. It was bad enough that she had placed herself in a position where she had to be rescued by this man, but now to display such ridiculous weakness. All she was doing was confirming that she didn't have the stamina for the job she had been sent to do. She was condemning herself before she even got to see Professor Morgan.

'Here.' He produced an immaculate linen handkerchief from his pocket and passed it to her.

'Thank you,' she managed.

He grinned maliciously. 'What restraint! Why don't you fling it at me, and damn me to hell for good measure? Women with your colouring aren't usually so placid under adversity.'

She dried her eyes, forcing herself to speak normally. 'You've known so many, of course.'

'My fair share,' he said laconically. 'And as we've moved on to a personal level—how many men have you known?'

Suddenly the picture of James was large in her mind. It had not occurred to her until then that he might be back at the Institute, returned from whatever mission he had been carrying out for the expedition. She felt a cold chill at the thought. She could imagine the image she presented at that moment—tangled hair, eyes red and blurred with weeping. Her appearance, quite apart from the mess she had all unwittingly landed herself in, would be a total affront to his tidy soul.

'You're very quiet,' he commented laconically. 'Are you

searching your memory or simply freezing me with your silence?'

The colour rose in her face as she recalled what his original question had been.

'I was thinking about something else,' she said lamely.

'It figures. You have plenty to think about.' He glanced at her. 'Have you given any further consideration to going home?'

She thought of the empty, immaculate flat and shivered a little. 'Where is home?' she said, almost inaudibly. But he heard her.

'What does the old cliché say? Home is where the heart is. To put it in more manageable terms—with your family —your friends.'

'I—I have no family.' It felt like the truth, she thought desolately, clenching her ringless left hand in the folds of her skirt.

'Miss Lonelyhearts herself.' His voice was smooth and mocking. 'Is this why you've come to the Yucatan, Miss Christow? In the hopes of finding someone to play Tarzan to your Jane in the rain forest?'

She flinched. 'No, Dr Lennox,' she said tightly. 'I came because my interest in the Maya is as serious as your own, and I'd be grateful if you'd stop treating me as if I was some silly child . . .'

'Is that how I've been treating you?' His smile widened. 'I can assure you I don't see you in that light at all.'

Her head was aching slightly. She put up her hand and pushed her hair back. Her fingers felt warm and a little clammy. She thought longingly of a cool shower and some food.

'I'm tired of all this verbal fencing, Dr Lennox,' she said wearily. 'I realise, of course, that you're quite determined that I shouldn't accompany this expedition, but I can't find any adequate reason for your opposition.'

'Can't you?' She felt his glance on her.

'No. You can't pretend, for instance, that women never go. Are you saying that you wouldn't take part in an expedition that included women?'

'Certainly not,' he drawled. 'There are some women I'd be quite happy to include.'

'But not me.' Anger was taking its grip on her. 'Will you please tell me why—why there should be one rule for "some women" and another for me?'

He pulled the jeep over to the side of the road and switched off the engine. It was too dark to see him properly. Everything was very quiet suddenly, and his voice was part of the quietness.

'You really want to know? You really want one good reason why I shouldn't take you into the rain forest?'

'Yes,' she said shakily, her mouth suddenly dry with an apprehension she did not fully understand.

Hands like steel bands took hold of her shoulders, impelling her towards him, so hard and so fast that she did not have time even to utter a protest. His mouth was warm on hers, without gentleness, a bruising menace in the darkness. She tried to resist after the first panic-stricken seconds of rigidity to pull away, but his arms were shackles holding her against him, her breasts crushed against the hard strength of his chest. Every nerve she possessed was screaming with shock. No one—not even James in their courting days, and certainly not later in that mockery of a marriage—had ever kissed her like this, parting her lips with dangerous sensuality, forcing her into this terrifying intimacy. Each time she tried to break free, his kiss merely deepened. She could feel his hands on her back, moving tantalisingly over her shoulders and down the shuddering length of her spine. She could feel their warmth through her thin shirt and knew with a shock of utter dismay that she wanted to feel them on her skin . . .

He let her go so suddenly that her head swam and she was glad to lean back against the seat, gasping for breath, her eyes partly closed as she fought for self-control against the traitorous longing to turn to him again, offering him her mouth and more.

'Now do you see why?' His voice sounded completely toneless. 'Do you understand why it's impossible for you to come with us?'

She had almost forgotten she was being taught a lesson. She shrank inside, thanking any listening God that she had not betrayed to him that sudden wild urge to respond.

'Because you can't be trusted not to behave like—an animal!' The words came tensely from her swollen mouth and she raised her fingers tentatively to touch it.

'Hardly an animal,' he drawled. 'Merely a human male—allowing for the fact that the rain forest brings out the primitive element in most of us. And I wouldn't be the only one, Gabrielle. There wouldn't be a man on that expedition who wouldn't be looking at that lovely face of yours and watching the way your body moves inside those demure clothes you wear, and wondering what you'd look like without them. And when someone got to find out—which he would do, eventually—then the trouble would really start. I've seen the havoc that some women can cause, and I don't intend this expedition to fall to pieces because of you.'

She was shivering violently. 'You've missed out on one important calculation, Dr Lennox—by denigrating me as some sort of sexual push-over. Don't you believe I'm capable of holding unwanted admirers at arm's length?'

'On tonight's showing—frankly, no.'

'You took me by surprise.' Her voice shook. 'I can promise you it will never happen again.'

'Do you want to bet?' he said evenly. 'I'm quite prepared to wager a year's salary that if I turned this jeep now and went back to Hernandez' place and took that room, we'd still be in bed together twenty-four hours from now.'

'You are utterly vile!' she whispered.

'Is that what that icy little brain of yours is telling you,

Gabrielle?' Even in the darkness, she knew he was smiling. 'Well, your body tells me a different story. But, under the circumstances I'm going to pretend I don't hear it and drive you to the Institute.'

Her brain was whirling, wildly, crazily as he re-started the engine and the jeep moved forward again. She would protest about his behaviour at the Institute. She would tell Professor Morgan how his trusted deputy behaved. But what could she complain about? He had only kissed her, and there was no law forbidding an unattached man to kiss an unattached girl. Only she wasn't unattached—was she? Her hands gripped tightly together in her lap. It was her own fault for pretending. She should have made it clear from the start that she was married to James. It was something she would put right as soon as they got to the Institute—whether James was there or not.

But there was no comfort in the thought, or even security. Instead she felt a bewildering sense of alienation —almost of loss—settling bleakly on her during the remainder of the drive.

CHAPTER THREE

GABRIELLE glanced round her room and uttered a sigh that mixed relief with contentment. Her surroundings were more practical than luxurious, but just at that moment she would not have exchanged them for a five-star hotel.

Professor Morgan's greeting had been warm enough, but it was clear to Gabrielle that he shared Shaun Lennox's view of her unsuitability. He was a tall man with a shock of hair and a greying beard, and a markedly piercing gaze was masked slightly by the rimless glasses he wore. Gabrielle had intended identifying herself at once as James Warner's wife, but she was given no chance to explain. After welcoming her briefly, the Professor handed her over to his wife to deal with, and it was Grace Morgan who had conducted her to the first floor and shown Gabrielle her room with its tiled floor and white-covered bed. She had been delighted to see the little shower compartment that opened out of it and Grace had smiled understandingly at the longing look she had sent it.

But her attempt to explain exactly who she was and justify her presence in Merida was cut short. Grace lifted a smiling hand, silencing her rather disjointed words.

'No explanations now, my dear. You've had an unpleasant day, I'm afraid, but we'll try and make it up to you—while you're here,' she added rather awkwardly. 'Make yourself at home, and I'll send Pepita up in about twenty minutes to bring you down to the dining room.'

The shower was bliss, and it was wonderful to change into clean undies and the simple black dress she had brought with her for evening wear and brush her hair until her scalp tingled. Her last act was to retrieve the little box from her case and slip her wedding ring on to her finger. It felt cold and strange and she was conscious of it all the time as she accompanied Pepita downstairs.

The room into which she was shown was quite crowded and she paused in the doorway, her heart pounding, searching the group for James' dapper figure. By the time she had assimilated that he was not there, Professor Morgan had reached her side and was introducing her to members of the nearest group. Gabrielle's head was soon whirling as she tried to remember names and areas of responsibility and link them with faces. It was a cosmopolitan organisation, with British and Americans predominating, but there were also a number of Mexicans and several Frenchmen. There were few women beside herself and Grace Morgan. The only one to hold a position of any importance was Dr Anna Lang, a calm-faced woman in her early forties who seemed to live in a permanent dream world occupied by the glyphs which were her passion. The others were the wives of archaeologists attached to the Institute, and Gabrielle felt bleak as she shook hands with them. It seemed there had been nothing to prevent James bringing her to Merida with him after all—nothing but his own lack of inclination. She had tried to excuse him by telling herself that it was consideration for her comfort which had prompted him to leave her behind. But although conditions at the Institute might be Spartan in some ways, yet they were far from the primitive level that James had managed to convey in the few discussions they had had on the matter.

Gabrielle was so engrossed in her own thoughts that Professor Morgan had almost completed the round of introductions before she realised he was still calling her Miss Christow. She felt hot with embarrassment at the thought of having to confess her true identity. She would have to find some less public moment, she thought desperately.

Dinner was a delicious experience, soup with meat balls being followed by steak accompanied by mashed avocado and fried beans. Gabrielle felt totally replete when she laid down her knife and fork, and she smilingly refused the fruit which was offered as dessert.

'I couldn't,' she apologised to Grace Morgan. 'Many more meals like this and I shall have to let out all my seams or buy a new wardrobe!'

Grace nodded. 'Yes, we have a good cook. But I don't think you need worry about your figure, my dear. You could add a few pounds, I think. And as for buying new clothes, I hope you don't mean to go home without buying yourself at least one *ipil*. They're the pretty embroidered smocks the women wear here,' she continued in answer to Gabrielle's questioning glance. 'They're long enough to wear as a dress if your legs are good enough to take a short skirt. Mine aren't any longer,' she added regretfully.

Gabrielle had tensed slightly at the casual reference to her possibly imminent departure, but she made herself relax and respond to Grace Morgan's genuine friendliness.

'I haven't had much chance yet to look at the shops,' she admitted.

Grace smiled at her warmly. 'Then you mustn't miss the Mercado Municipal. They sell everything there. We must assign someone to take you around. Perhaps Shaun ...' She glanced around as if she was looking for him and Gabrielle was shocked into speech.

'Oh, please, I can manage quite well alone. I don't want to put Dr Lennox to any more trouble on my account,' she protested, feeling the betraying colour flood her cheeks.

Grace Morgan gave her a puzzled look. 'Well, of course not. I hardly intended—I mean, Shaun has been so busy what with Dennis' illness and everything else. I really don't think he would have the time to do any sightseeing. All I thought was that he might know someone who could take you about. I'd do so myself, but I act as Dennis' secretary.'

Gabrielle mentally berated herself for her own stupidity.

As if she could imagine Shaun Lennox acting as her guide anyway while she window-shopped! It was a ludicrous thought.

Coffee was served in the long, low room which was used as a common recreation area by all members of the Institute. The long patio doors stood open to the courtyard that Gabrielle remembered and she could hear the faint splash of the fountain. There was no breeze blowing in through the sliding wire-mesh screens that prevented the intrusion of insects into the lighted room, and Gabrielle was glad of the big electric fans which whirred ceaselessly from the ceiling. She found a tissue in her bag and unobtrusively blotted a few beads of perspiration from her temples and upper lip.

'Feeling the humidity, Miss Christow?' a faintly jeering voice asked close to her ear. 'Conditions here are pleasant compared to those in the rain forest, I promise you.'

Gabrielle stiffened, thrusting the tissue back into her bag. Shaun Lennox had not been present at the dinner, she had noted thankfully, but she supposed it was too much to hope that she would have got through the evening without meeting him again. The memory of what had so recently passed between them made it impossible for her simply to accept his presence with equanimity, however.

'You don't have to worry about me, Dr Lennox.' She hated the slight breathlessness in her voice. 'By the time the expedition leaves, I expect to be completely acclimatised.'

The slight satirical smile playing about his firm mouth widened at her words, but Gabrielle forestalled any possible reply by rising abruptly from her chair on the pretext of returning her empty cup to the table. She felt suddenly, desperately tired and a headache was threatening. She decided she would have a few minutes in whatever air there was in the courtyard before making her excuses and going to her room.

The screens slid easily aside at the touch of her hand and she slipped through the slight gap into the open. The feeling of peace and tranquillity she had sensed the previous day seemed even more pronounced in the heavy, scented darkness, and she breathed deeply, relaxing almost insensibly. A bird called suddenly from the flowers massed above her head on the verandah, a long piercing solitary trill that found no answer, and Gabrielle found herself shivering at the recollection of her own isolation.

She was almost glad to hear the other footfall on the wooden slats of the verandah behind her, even though she knew with a sense of inevitability who had followed her.

'You're very persistent, Dr Lennox,' she threw at him over her shoulder. There was a moment's silence, but her hope that she had taken him aback was short-lived.

'And you're very prone to leap to conclusions,' he said eventually and rather grimly. 'Dennis sent me to find you, as a matter of fact. He wants a word with you.'

She was glad the darkness hid her blazing cheeks.

'I see,' she mumbled. 'Thank you.'

'Por nada.' There was a further pause, then he said quietly, 'This can all stop now, if you want.'

'What do you mean?' All the soft, sweet sounds of the night seemed muffled compared with the uneven pounding of her heart.

'I mean'—his voice was level, 'that we could declare a truce for the short time you're here. Who knows? It could even prove—enjoyable.'

'I'm here to work, Dr Lennox.' She strove for the casual touch, but knew she had missed it by yards. 'Not to provide enjoyment—even for someone as eminent as you.'

'My God, you've got a nasty tongue,' he said softly. 'Is this your usual reaction to any man who shows you that he finds you desirable? Or is it just something about me that arouses your resentment?'

She moved her shoulders wearily, conscious that tears were not far away.

'I'd prefer not to discuss it,' she said tightly. 'Will you excuse me now, please. Professor Morgan will be waiting.'

But he made no attempt to move aside to allow her to pass him.

'There's no immediate hurry.' He folded his arms and studied her, his dark brows drawn together frowningly. 'You intrigue me, Gabrielle, with this determined imitation of an icicle. And it is an imitation—I'm sure of that, at least.'

A long wild shiver ran through her as if it were his hands rather than those piercing blue eyes that were making that long, practised head-to-toe assessment of her body in the clinging black dress.

She tilted her chin in a defiance she was far from feeling. 'The obvious explanation hasn't occurred to you, Dr Lennox. Perhaps I just don't find you attractive.'

'Perhaps not,' he returned equably. 'It's a theory it might be interesting to test, however.'

He took one long, considered stride towards her, and she stepped backwards, openly panicking, her fists clenching uncontrollably in the folds of her skirt.

'Don't—please!' She despised herself, for the tremor she could hear in her voice.

'If you're appealing to my better nature, Gabrielle—it doesn't exist.'

He paused, a mere matter of inches away from her, his hands resting lightly on his hips. He looked as dangerous and unpredictable as one of the jungle cats, and the verandah rail was touching her back. There was nowhere for her to retreat to.

She said breathlessly, 'Do you treat all your women colleagues in this way, Dr Lennox?'

He smiled faintly. 'No—but then you aren't a woman colleague.'

She bit her lip. 'And—and are your colleagues' wives also sacrosanct?'

'Naturally.' A certain hardness had entered his voice. 'Why do you ask?'

Mutely, she extended her left hand. The pale glimmer of her ring caught his attention immediately.

'Very pretty. Is it real—or just a form of insurance against unwanted advances?'

'It's real,' she said quietly.

'I see.' Physically he hadn't moved an inch, yet he suddenly seemed utterly remote. 'You must have an amazingly tolerant husband. Or doesn't he care that you've come halfway across the world to risk your life with a bunch of complete strangers?'

'It isn't like that . . .'

'Oh? Then tell me how it is, Gabrielle. Tell me about this fantastic marriage that can still function across two continents.' The vivid blue eyes went over her again, and she quailed inwardly at the blaze of anger in their depths. 'I'd like to meet this singular husband of yours and find out just what makes him tick. How he can bear to have you out of his sight—and out of his arms—for even five minutes, let alone the months this assignment is likely to take, is beyond my comprehension.'

A bubble of hysteria welled up inside her. 'It's a good question, Dr Lennox. Perhaps we can both ask him that—when he comes back?'

'What the hell do you mean?'

'You haven't asked my married name yet,' she flung at him. 'Would it help if I told you it was Warner?'

It was out at last, not in the way or at the time she had envisaged, but a relief just the same.

His eyes narrowed to sapphire chips. He gripped her arm, his roughness bruising the soft flesh.

'You're—James Warner's wife?' He bit the words out.

'Yes, Dr Lennox.' With a curious detachment, she noticed how sharply defined the planes and angles of his narrow face suddenly seemed, the high cheekbones more prominent than ever, the firm lips tightened to an angry slash.

He swore briefly and shockingly, then turned and began to stride along the verandah, pulling her with him.

'Where are we going?' She tried to twist free, but his grip on her was as inflexible—and impersonal—as a handcuff.

'To find Dennis.' He did not look at her. 'Or was this amazing piece of information supposed to remain our little secret?'

She shrank at the note of suppressed fury that underran the jibe in his voice.

She was left on her own in Professor Morgan's private office while Shaun Lennox went off to find the older man. She sank trembling on to the nearest of the high-backed chairs which fronted the big desk. She hadn't meant to blurt it all out like that, she thought despairingly. It was all the fault of that Lennox man—disturbing her, provoking her, getting under her skin. Her hands twisted together. How ironic and how hurtful that he should have asked her the very question she had tormented herself with so many times in London. How could James accept their separation?

The bitterness of her reverie was interrupted by Professor Morgan's grave 'Mrs Warner?' from the doorway.

She glanced up, trying to summon a wan smile to her trembling mouth.

'I'm sorry, Professor. I realise I should have told you immediately ...'

'Yes, I think you should.' He came across the room and stood looking down at her, his face troubled.

'You see—I was expecting James to be here. I didn't know what to do.'

'James knew you were coming?'

'Didn't he mention it?'

'No, he didn't, or we'd have tried to organise a very different sort of welcome.'

'But I wrote to him—twice.' A sense of desolation tightened her throat as she realised all her worst forebodings had been correct.

Professor Morgan walked over to his desk and unlocked one of the drawers. He withdrew a handful of letters, fastened with a rubber band, and selected two with airmail markings. He held them out to her in silence. She looked down at them in disbelief.

'But they haven't been opened.'

'No. They both came after James had left here.'

'But couldn't they have been sent on?'

'Of course—if we had known where he was.'

She stared up at him, the colour draining out of her face. 'I don't understand.'

'Don't you, Mrs Warner?' Shaun Lennox strolled forward and perched himself on the edge of the Professor's desk. 'We were hoping you could help us understand.'

'I'm sorry.' She pressed weary fingers against her hectically throbbing temples. 'I don't . . .'

'You came to meet James,' he said softly. 'But he isn't here, so what's your next move going to be?'

'My—next move, as you put it, Dr Lennox, will be to get on with the work I've been sent here to do. I can promise you that my—personal difficulties won't make any difference . . .' She got no further.

'God, but you're cool!' He swung to Professor Morgan with a short, mirthless laugh. 'Her husband has disappeared—off the face of the earth for all anyone knows—and her sole concern is with this phoney magazine assignment!'

'Disappeared?' It was her turn to appeal to the silent Professor. 'I thought James was working somewhere else temporarily—Villahermosa, perhaps.'

'You knew he'd been to Villahermosa?' Was it her imagination, she wondered, or had his eyes suddenly become watchful behind those masking lenses?

'One of the girls in the office—Isabella—mentioned it. She said he'd been there with you.' She looked at Shaun Lennox.

'She's quite right. You haven't wasted much time, have you?' Shaun Lennox took a cigarette from a box on the desk and lit it, his eyes cold as they met hers across the lighter flame. 'I was there with—Dr Warner a while back. I left him there and no one has seen him or heard from him since.'

'But why not?' She looked from one to the other, her eyes wide with shock. 'Wouldn't it have been more usual for him to have returned here?'

'Perhaps.' Shaun Lennox drew deeply on the cigarette. 'But you see, Mrs Warner, there was some—trouble in Villahermosa.'

'What kind of trouble?'

He lifted one shoulder almost casually. 'I suppose you could say we quarrelled.'

'I—see.' Looking at him, she thought she did. There was no way in which a clash of personalities between these two men could have been avoided. Shaun Lennox and his abrasive modernity opposed to James' old-fashioned, even pedantic approach. Even the common ground of their interest in Mayan history would not have been sufficient to reconcile them.

'Are you all right, Mrs Warner?' Professor Morgan's voice sounded a long way off, grave and impersonal. 'Shaun, perhaps some brandy. Ask my wife ...'

'No.' Gabrielle lifted her hand, forcing herself back to reality, to this quiet room and the odd hostility which seemed to surround her. 'I'm fine. It was just rather a shock. You've really no idea where James is now?'

'How odd,' Shaun Lennox said almost idly. 'I was just

going to ask you the same thing.'

Her eyes widened with shock. 'But I've already told you —I thought he would be here.' She almost said 'waiting for me', but her inherent truthfulness would not permit it.

'You see, Mrs Warner,' it was the Professor again, 'we're in rather a difficult position. On the one hand there is James, about whom we are naturally anxious. Now you turn up, first of all claiming to be the magazine representative we've been expecting, and now stating you are James' wife.'

'Did James never mention me?' It was odd how little pain the question cost her.

'Oh, we knew he was married, of course. We've known for some considerable time. But somehow we'd gleaned a rather different image.' He looked at her doubtfully. 'We had no idea, for instance, that you were involved in photographic journalism.'

Gabrielle was silent. She was reluctant even at this stage to reveal the true circumstances of her marriage, particularly to Shaun Lennox. It would be humiliating to have to explain just how poor the level of communication between James and herself had been. She lifted her head and looked steadily at Professor Morgan.

'It is—rather a new venture for me.'

Shaun Lennox expelled a long, impatient breath. 'I thought as much.'

'But I'm perfectly well qualified for the assignment.' She glared at him. 'Do you really imagine *Vision* would have sent me here if I was as incompetent as you seem to insinuate?'

Professor Morgan sighed, pushing his glasses up on to his forehead. 'No doubt you have credentials, Mrs Warner.'

For a moment she did not understand, then Shaun Lennox elaborated with a kind of icy patience, 'Proof, Mrs Warner. Proof that you are who you say you are and that you can actually perform what you claim.'

She got to her feet. 'Would you also like to see my marriage certificate?' she asked, her voice shaking with anger.

'Perhaps it wouldn't be a bad idea,' he drawled.

She didn't know quite what she expected Professor Morgan's reaction to be. Perhaps a rebuke to Dr Lennox—an apology to herself. But he remained silent, staring frowningly down at the polished surface of his desk.

She felt cold all over. Anger mingled with fright and bewilderment. This was worse than any of the events that had preceded it since her arrival in Merida. They didn't believe her. With Shaun Lennox it was almost understandable. Between them, it was some kind of strange war to the death—of what? Self-respect, perhaps, her mind said wildly as she tried to compose her tumbling thoughts.

She said very quietly, when she could trust herself to speak, 'I'll go and get the papers you require.'

Upstairs, she met Grace Morgan. 'My dear, I've been looking for you everywhere,' the older woman began. 'Surely Dennis and Shaun aren't spoiling your first evening here with business talk. It's too bad of them, especially . . .' She broke off awkwardly.

'Especially as it's unlikely that I'll be staying, anyway,' Gabrielle finished for her, smiling through oddly stiff lips. 'It's all right, Mrs Morgan. It's more a preliminary interrogation than a business chat.' She went past into her room, closing the door behind her and leaning against the panels for a moment while she fought for her self-control.

Her document wallet lay at the bottom of her case, and she jerked it out, sending clothes flying. She looked down at them almost contemptuously—the hard-wearing denims and cottons that she had brought for the actual trip into the rain forest. They wouldn't be needed now.

The cardboard folder clutched in her hand, she flung open her bedroom door and marched out, almost cannoning into Shaun Lennox.

'I'm so *sorry*!' Her voice was almost hysterically sarcastic. 'Did I take too long? Were you afraid I was up here, cooking the evidence or something?'

He took her by the shoulders. 'Cool it,' he advised succinctly. 'This has been one hell of a day and I'm in no mood for female histrionics at this stage of it. But I'll promise you this, Miss Christow—or Mrs Warner or whatever you feel like calling yourself. Any outsider who came here would be questioned and asked for some means of identification. We have good reason for being ultra-careful, believe me.'

'I do believe you.' She made herself speak more calmly. 'I just wish you'd do me the same courtesy.'

He put one hand forcefully under her chin, making her look up and meet his gaze.

'What's eating you? The fact that we've cast doubt on your married state? God in heaven, Gabrielle, do I have to spell it out to you? James and you!' He shook his head. 'Do you wonder people find it incredible.'

'You're insulting,' she whispered.

'I'm a realist. And I've known a few women in my time.' The blue eyes roved relentlessly over her white face. 'Married women—the happy ones, that is—have an aura about them—a warmth and softness in their faces that loving and being loved brings. You don't have that, Gabrielle.' He let one finger trace her cheekbones and the vulnerable line of her jaw. 'In spite of your gold ring and your marriage lines, you don't look like a wife.'

'How dare you!' She tore herself away from him, every nerve in her body taut and screaming at his proximity.

A sudden vision of the flat forced itself relentlessly into her mind's eye. The carefully lit statuary, the locked show-cases. She felt herself shiver, then rallied her defences.

'It may surprise you to learn, Dr Lennox, that we don't all conduct our relationships on a purely animal level.' Deliberately she fought away the memory of her hurt and bewilderment as the utter sterility of her marriage had come home to her. 'There are other aspects of marriage which may not have occurred to you. There's a spiritual side to it—a—comradeship. A sharing of interests.'

'Bravo,' he applauded ironically. 'And was it part of this comradely sharing that caused you to be left behind in London—why you had to seize on some magazine assignment as an excuse to come out here? It doesn't sound like comradeship to me, Gabrielle. It sounds like desperation.'

'James understands,' she insisted wildly. 'Women aren't just satellites, you know. We have lives of our own—careers of our own.'

His satirical smile widened. 'Can we be speaking of the same Dr Warner? Go on, Gabrielle.' He stood aside so that she could pass him. 'Go down to Dennis and convince him of your good faith. He may be more gullible than I am, but I doubt it.'

'Don't you intend to escort me back to his door?' she asked, stung.

'No.' His lids drooped lazily over his eyes as he looked her over. 'I don't see myself as a tame escort. There are some husbandly rights that even I don't intend to usurp. Goodnight, Gabrielle, although I suppose it would be more correct to say—goodbye.'

He turned and moved away with that quick, lithe stride. Gabrielle stood and watched him go, one hand pressed to her throat. Then she turned and went back into her room, going straight to the dressing chest and the mirror that surmounted it. A stranger looked back at her, with a taut, white face and green eyes as wary as a cat's, a spot of colour burning on each cheekbone. The face of a girl who had been given one fleeting glimpse of what fulfilment could mean and then had it snatched away from her for ever.

'Damn you, Shaun Lennox,' she thought savagely, as tears blurred the mirrored image. 'Damn you to hell!'

Gabrielle sat on a cane seat in a shaded part of the verandah, trying to concentrate on the book that lay open in her lap. Permission to use the library had been one of the few concessions that had come her way since she had arrived at the Institute two days before, she thought wryly. Even though she had succeeded in establishing her identity and credentials with Professor Morgan, she was still very much an outsider. People were polite, careful to include her in general conversations at mealtimes, yet she had very little real idea of the type of work that went on at the Institute and her hesitant inquiry as to whether she could take some preliminary pictures of some of the expedition members had been firmly vetoed.

In fact, no one seemed prepared to discuss the expedition or any aspect of it with her at all. Gabrielle sighed and pushed the book aside. Reading about the towering pyramids of Tikal, or the enormous ball court at Chichen Itza, was no longer enough now that she was actually here, and all these wonders were at least within striking distance.

But she still had no idea whether Professor Morgan was prepared to accept her as *Vision*'s representative and take her with them. All the arrangements were going ahead. In spite of her exclusion from them, she could sense the growing excitement and feeling of tension at the Institute. Even the placid-looking Dr Lang was showing signs of eager animation.

Everything served to emphasise Gabrielle's own sense of isolation, she thought bitterly. She was the unwanted guest in the busy household, the gatecrasher at the party.

The only satisfaction from her point of view was Shaun Lennox's continuing absence. Casual remarks from some of the others revealed that he had gone to Mexico City, and Gabrielle hoped that if she had to leave Merida, she could do so without meeting him again. The memory of their last confrontation still disturbed her profoundly. And it was not just that he was so frank about the physical attraction she had for him, she told herself vehemently. Other men had flirted with her, but their attentions had been something to be enjoyed and parried lightly. None of them had ever reduced her to such quivering tension.

And if he did return soon, at least these few days' respite had given her a chance to recover her poise, she told herself stoutly. He would not find her such easy prey for his mocking barbs again.

She got up, shaking the creases impatiently out of her skirt. She would do better to relegate Shaun Lennox to the back of her mind permanently and concentrate on the problem of James' whereabouts, she thought, trying to stifle the sense of guilt that assailed her each time she thought of her husband. There was still no word from him or about him, and none of his colleagues at the Institute seemed prepared to speculate where he was or what he was doing. The only reassuring note had been struck by Professor Morgan, who opined that James had gone ahead to the base camp which was being set up, and which was not yet in radio contact with the Institute headquarters.

From what she could gather, the base camp was a collection of prefabricated dwellings occupying a specially cleared site in the rain forest, an oasis of semi-civilisation to which the expedition members could return for much-needed rest. For one thing, there were dormitory huts with proper camp beds, instead of the hammocks that would be used in the forest itself, as well as a medical centre, a laboratory and research area, including—Gabrielle sighed again—a darkroom. She wandered moodily over to the verandah rail and stood staring across the courtyard at the fountain.

If James was at the camp, wouldn't word have filtered back somehow? And somehow she could hardly visualise him sweating somewhere, setting up facilities for other people. Looking back over their brief married life, it seemed more likely that he had withdrawn somewhere to sulk after his quarrel with Dr Lennox. She pushed a tendril of hair wearily back from her face. It was always possible that James' habit of taking refuge in icy silences when displeased had been reserved for their relationship alone, but she doubted it. Looking back, it seemed an ingrained part of his nature, and she was forced to admit that whatever the rights or wrongs of his disagreement with Dr Lennox, James would not be an easy person to have as a colleague. The other members' obvious reluctance to discuss him with her seemed to indicate a certain lack of popularity, she thought unhappily.

Of one thing she was sure. James' devotion to Mayan exploration would force him to join the expedition at some stage. All she had to do now was persuade Professor Morgan that she had a double right to go with them, both as James' wife and *Vision*'s accredited representative, and sooner or later they would be reunited. In spite of the heat of the day, her hands felt suddenly cold and clammy and she wiped them on her skirt, smoothing the material over her thighs. Already her life with James was taking on a dreamlike quality. There were times, as now, when she found it difficult to remember his physical presence, his features, and had to build them carefully as a witness might choose items for an Identi-kit, she thought wonderingly. She tried to assemble James in her mind, the immaculate clothes, the trim beard, the small, rather prim mouth. But the eyes were wrong, she thought wonderingly. They were blue and vivid, set under slanting brows. She stifled a cry as she realised the image that her mind was re-creating. She would not think of that man. She would not. She was James' wife. Until they could meet and talk and decide what the future held for them, if anything, then at least she owed him the total commitment she had promised when they were married. There was loyalty too. Shaun Lennox, it seemed clear, was no friend to James. It was wrong—it was a form of infidelity to permit them to clash again for the unconscious possession of her thoughts.

She started violently as a voice behind her said, '*Señorita?*' Swinging round, she discovered Isabella regarding her unsmilingly.

'Yes?' Gabrielle moistened her lips.

'There is a telephone call.' Isabella turned away, assuming that Gabrielle would follow.

'A call for me?' Gabrielle's heart gave a painful thump. Could it be James making contact at last? 'Did—did the caller give a name?'

'*No.*' Isabella shrugged. 'But it is a man, *señorita.* Oh, *dispénseme,* maybe I should say *señora, no*?'

Gabrielle ignored the provocative rudeness in the girl's tone.

'Er—where do I take the call—in the office?' she asked.

'It is permitted.' Isabella moved off with her slightly swaying walk and Gabrielle followed her reluctantly. If it was James waiting on the other end of the telephone, she would rather their first conversation was not overheard by Isabella and the others, but she supposed with the number of people who worked at the Institute any kind of privacy would be at a premium anyway.

The other girls were working busily at typewriters when Gabrielle came in, and they merely exchanged rather shy smiles with her before returning their attention to their work. But Isabella flounced into a chair, rather sulkily indicating the extension that Gabrielle should use for her call, and Gabrielle realised with exasperation that she was going to have an audience. She picked up the receiver, feeling awkward.

'Hello?'

'Is that you, Gabrielle?'

James had never sounded so exuberant on the phone, she

realised with a traitorous sense of relief.

The voice went on, 'Gee, you sound thrown! I bet Cathy you wouldn't know who it was. Have I rung at a bad time?'

With a rush of pleasure, Gabrielle placed the voice. It was Jon Benson, the pleasant American she had met at the hotel.

'No, Jon. It's—it's lovely to hear from you. How are you both?'

'Just great. We thought we'd give you time to settle in before we started to bombard you with calls. Cathy reckoned they might have your nose to the grindstone already. Is it O.K. to talk?'

'Yes, fine. I just didn't expect to hear from you, that's all.'

'Now we did promise. The thing is, Gabrielle, we're planning a final trip before we head home, and we're going to drive to Chichen Itza tomorrow. How about going with us?'

Gabrielle gave a gasp of genuine delight. 'Oh, Jon, that would be wonderful! Are you sure you don't mind? I don't want to play gooseberry or anything.'

'You're the best-looking gooseberry I ever saw,' Jon laughed. 'We'd both love to have you along. Can you get the time off?'

'Oh, yes.' Gabrielle realised that both Jon and Cathy imagined she was an accepted member of the expedition by now. 'There—there'll be no trouble about that.'

'That's great. Cath reckons we ought to make an early start. It's about a seventy-mile trip, so what say we pick you up at the Institute just before eight tomorrow?'

Gabrielle accepted happily. Jon's open friendliness and the prospect of a trip to one of the Mayan sites which most appealed to her imagination were a potent combination, and she was smiling as she replaced the receiver.

'You have friends in Merida, *señora*?'

Gabrielle turned to meet Isabella's speculative gaze.

Her brows lifted slightly. 'Some people I met at the hotel,' she replied quietly. 'Is it important?'

Isabella shrugged. 'Just that you are not alone here as the *señor* director thought.'

The implication was obvious, Gabrielle realised, her temper rising. Isabella thought she had obtained accommodation at the Institute through false pretences.

'The *señor* director knows all the circumstances of my being in Merida,' she said, aware that her colour was heightened. 'Perhaps you should direct any criticism of my being here to him.'

Isabella spread her hands exaggeratedly. 'It is not for me to criticise, *señora*,' she replied. 'I am, after all, only an employee.'

'Perhaps you should remember that,' Gabrielle said coldly, and left the room.

On the way up to her own room, she met Grace Morgan who gave her a slightly harassed smile, and asked if everything was all right.

'Fine, thanks,' Gabrielle returned with more determination than truth. 'I shall be happier when I have something to do, however.'

Mrs Morgan sighed. 'Such a difficult position to be in ... I'm sure my husband will reach a decision soon, my dear.'

'I hope so.' Gabrielle gave her a faint smile. 'In the meantime, I think I'll have a wander round the street markets you mentioned.'

'You're going out?' Gabrielle was sure she hadn't imagined a look of sudden consternation in Mrs Morgan's eyes. 'Oh, my dear, are you sure that's wise? On your own in a city you don't know and in the hottest part of the day.'

Gabrielle gave her a puzzled look. 'I shan't walk too far,' she said slowly. 'But I feel I must do something. I'm not used to just sitting around. I feel so useless.'

'Couldn't you postpone your trip until tomorrow? Then I could come with you, perhaps,' Mrs Morgan suggested.

Gabrielle's bewilderment grew. 'That's not possible, I'm afraid,' she said. 'Some acquaintances from the hotel have arranged to take me to Chichen Itza with them.'

Mrs Morgan's worried expression seemed to increase. 'You're going to Chichen Itza? Oh, dear. Have you mentioned this to Dennis?'

'No.' Gabrielle stared at her. 'Surely—I mean, I didn't think I needed anyone's *permission* before accepting the invitation.'

'No, of course, you wouldn't. Heavens, how difficult everything is.' Mrs Morgan appeared to be talking to herself. 'I suppose it's too late to postpone the excursion, as well.'

'I'm afraid it is.' Gabrielle's patience, already sorely tried by the encounter with Isabella, began to give way. 'After all, Mrs Morgan, it isn't as if I'm neglecting any of my duties here. As you know, I haven't any. I never imagined there would be any objection as to how I spent my own time.'

'Oh, no, of course not.' Mrs Morgan gave her a swift glance, then patted Gabrielle's arm with a placatory smile. 'It's just that we—Dennis—feels responsible for you.'

'I assure you, I can look after myself,' Gabrielle declared, pushing the memory of what had happened at the Hernandez bar firmly to the furthermost recesses of her mind.

Mrs Morgan's rather extraordinary attitude to her harmless shopping expedition and sightseeing trip continued to nag at her thoughts, however, even the following day as the Bensons' car wound out of the city through the flat grey-green *henequen* fields punctuated with the windmills that provided them with their water. She might not be the Institute's most welcome guest, but there was no reason why she should be treated as a prisoner, she told herself rebelliously. She was determined not to allow any of these problems to spoil her day out, and she was soon joining in Jon and Cathy's lighthearted bickering as to whether it was worth taking a slight detour to see the pirate Jean Lafitte's grave at Dzilan Bravo.

'On the way back, maybe,' Jon decided finally. 'We could stop over somewhere. You don't have to get back tonight, do you, Gabrielle?'

Gabrielle hesitated. The prospect of spending a night outside the confines of the Institute was an attractive one, but she had an uneasy feeling that the Morgans would oppose the idea, and she did not want to upset them while there was still a chance she would be allowed to accompany the expedition.

Cathy punched his arm good-humouredly. 'Grow up! She's a working girl. They'll expect her back, slaving over a hot camera, first thing tomorrow.'

Gabrielle nodded and smiled constrainedly, refraining from comment.

The car sped on, making the best of the so-called highway as it wound its way through a succession of villages, with little to distinguish the next one from the last. It was already very hot, and the dust rose in swirls from the roadside as they passed, making it impossible to have the car windows open and enjoy what little breeze their speed engendered.

It was a relief when they finally saw the towering grey stones rising slowly out of the plain ahead of them, and Gabrielle felt a stirring of excitement in the pit of her stomach. Photographs in books had only given her a glimpse of the reality, she thought, gripping her own camera more tightly.

Although it was still quite early in the day, there were already a number of tourists there, some obviously there for the day like themselves, and others who were staying at the nearby *haciendas* which catered for such traffic.

Gabrielle had been rather afraid that Jon and Cathy

might want to dash from building to building with herself scampering in their wake, but like everyone else, they seemed taken aback by the heat. The slightest movement seemed to send rivulets of perspiration running down Gabrielle's back, and they were glad to saunter quietly between the ruins and the neat emerald lawns which surrounded them, making the most of whatever shade offered. Besides, there was an air of hushed grandeur about the old Toltec city which seemed to have a sobering effect on visitors. Raised voices, or even the laughter of children, would have seemed totally out of place here, Gabrielle realised with an uncomfortable tingle along her nerve endings.

'I thought it would be bigger somehow,' Cathy said, training her own camera on the Castillo, its grey bulk dominating the central area. 'Everything seems kind of scaled down—especially after Palenque.'

John nodded. 'I know what you mean, hon, but it's got something just the same—something that puts a chill in your bones. Shall we go inside and take a look at this temple? It'll be cooler for one thing and we can get away from these darned flies,' he added, taking an irritable swipe at his neck.

Cathy turned to Gabrielle. 'We both have this cream that's supposed to be repellent to flies and mosquitoes. We know it, and the makers know it, only no one seems to have told the flies and mosquitoes!'

Gabrielle laughed and sympathised, and they went into the temple, bending slightly as they negotiated the rather squat doorway. The great red jaguar throne, encrusted with jade, glowed in the dim interior light. The flint fangs gleamed in the snarling mouth.

'I take back all I said.' There was awe in Cathy's voice when she eventually broke the silence. 'That is a tremendous thing. It—it's the colour of blood.'

Gabrielle nodded slowly. 'It tends to spoil the picture

one has of the Maya before the Spanish Conquest. Most of the stuff I've read suggests they were very gentle and intellectual, but this is a violent, savage thing.'

Jon was beckoning them from a nearby doorway. 'This may not be the colour of blood, but something tells me it should be,' he said wryly.

They went along a short tunnel and found themselves in a smaller chamber, entirely dominated by a reclining stone figure, the flat inhumanity of its features accentuated by the ivory that had been used to depict them.

'What in the world is that?' Cathy asked.

'It's a Chacmool—a statue of the rain god Chac.' Gabrielle's background reading came to her assistance. 'Apparently they used them as sacrificial altars. When someone was sacrificed, his heart would be cut out by the priests and put in that trough.'

'You don't say.' Cathy wrinkled her nose fastidiously. 'I thought this was the place where they just drowned people.'

'They did that too.' Gabrielle hated the way the statue's ivory eyes seemed to stare inimically back at her. 'Chac demanded all kinds of sacrifice. They felt he had to be continually—placated, if you like, with blood.'

She gave a little smile. 'From what I've gathered, his influence is still pretty strong. When archaeologists were dredging out the Well of Sacrifice a few years ago, all kinds of odd things kept happening—dreadful, unseasonal weather, accidents to the equipment, even lives being endangered. The Mayan workmen claimed it was Chac protecting what was his.'

'I bet he could too.' Cathy gave a slight shiver and turned away. 'I think I'll go back to the flies. They suddenly seem—healthier and more agreeable somehow.'

Gabrielle's legs were aching, and every inch of clothing felt as if it were sticking to her body by the time they sat down to lunch on the verandah of a small restaurant near the gatehouse. They had climbed the steep flight of steps to the top of the Castillo, looking over Chichen Itza as, Jon observed, the *conquistadores* must have done centuries before as they commandeered the Temple of the Plumed Serpent for their fortress, and had wandered marvelling round the great green expanse of the Ball Court, where Mayan warriors had once vied with each other to butt rubber balls through two stone rings fixed high on the wall.

'So the losers got the chop, huh?' Jon gave the graphic pictures carved into the stone terrace of the court a moody look before he turned away. 'Some of the ball games I've watched lately could do with a rule like that.'

'And this afternoon we'll go and take a look at the Well of Sacrifice itself,' Cathy planned happily over the platters of *enchiladas*.

Jon groaned. 'I feel like a sacrifice myself—a burnt offering. Why don't we forget the whole thing and take a run down to the coast? There'll be a phone somewhere for Gabrielle to call up her boss and warn them not to expect her. Hell, everyone's entitled to a couple of days off now and then.'

Gabrielle sighed. 'Not when you haven't actually done any work yet,' she answered honestly. 'Thanks anyway, Jon, but you'd better count me out. Don't let me stop either of you, though. I can easily get a bus back to Merida.'

Cathy gave her an outraged look. 'I won't hear of such a thing. And we're not leaving yet. I want to see the Sacred Well, and if Jon doesn't want to come with us, he can stay here and sleep.'

Jon laid down his fork with a sigh of repletion. 'Suit yourself, honey, but if you fall in, don't holler for me to come and pull you out. I want no part of Chac or his sacred waterhole.'

'Men!' Cathy grumbled good-naturedly as they walked

away. 'No one but women would put up with them.' She glanced sideways at Gabrielle as she spoke and her voice took on a note of constraint. 'Gaby, feel free to tell me to mind my own business any time you like, but I couldn't help noticing you're wearing a wedding ring today. Yet when we first met, I could swear you weren't.'

Gabrielle hesitated. Cathy seemed a genuine person, warmhearted and friendly, but she was still a stranger in most respects, and Gabrielle quailed at the thought of taking her fully into her confidence.

'I am married,' she admitted quietly after a moment. 'But I suppose you could say we're—separated at the moment, and that's why I don't always wear my ring.'

'Well, it happens,' Cathy shrugged philosophically. 'I've been lucky, I guess, but I don't kid myself that everything lasts for ever. How can you hold them if they want to go?'

And how can you hold them if they've never been there at all? Gabrielle thought bitterly as they walked on along the raised sacred way that led to the Well of Sacrifice.

She was not prepared for its size. Her notions of a *cenote* had involved a steep-sided pit where water glimmered far below. But not this—this monstrous gaping hole, measuring more than a hundred feet across, its rocky sides pitted like fangs, with brown trees and vegetation reaching hungry roots down towards the beckoning water. And it did beckon. Her stomach constricted involuntarily as she thought of what it had beckoned in its time. Not the treasures—the unique ceramics, the jade ornaments, the precious beaten gold artefacts imported with such effort and worked with such skill in this goldless land. Not even the willing human sacrifices—the girls and youths who had considered it an honour to be chosen to propitiate the malevolent god of the well. It was the children—the babies and toddlers who had been given to the hungry waters in their hundreds, judging by the tiny bones and skulls that had been discovered in the muddy depths, and who must have gone to their deaths comprehending nothing but their own terror as the dark water closed over them.

She shivered as she turned away, leaving her camera still in its case. She needed no reminder in film of this place. She would always remember it. Moving unwarily, her foot found a pebble which moved under her sandal, throwing her off balance. She felt herself stagger and realised how near she was to the rim. Then her shoulders were gripped firmly and she was steadied until the sky and baked mud and gleaming water stopped their mad dance to the frenzied beating of her heart. Somewhere near at hand, she heard Cathy exclaim and come running. Dazedly she looked up into the dark face of her rescuer.

'Another virgin sacrifice for the god, Gabrielle?' Shaun Lennox' smile was mirthless as he looked down at her. 'From all points of view, it's rather late in the day for that, isn't it?'

CHAPTER FOUR

GABRIELLE'S green eyes were frankly disbelieving as they met his.

'You!' she whispered. 'But what are you doing here? You're in Mexico City . . .'

'I was,' he corrected urbanely. 'Now I'm here. Is there some reason why I shouldn't be?'

Gabrielle shook her head slowly. Her mouth felt dry suddenly.

'None at all, I suppose,' she replied tonelessly. 'Except that I can't imagine Chichen Itza attracting you particularly as an archaeological site any longer. It's been too fully excavated.'

Shaun Lennox smiled down at her, a smile that did nothing to relieve the hardness in his eyes. 'Perhaps,' he said. 'On the other hand, I'm wondering if it may not have one or two more secrets to divulge—if I'm patient.'

Cathy had been listening wide-eyed to this exchange, but now she broke in impatiently.

'Say, who are you anyway?'

Gabrielle saw a certain grimness entering Shaun's expression and intercepted hastily. 'Oh, of course you two haven't met. Cathy, this is Dr Lennox from the Institute—where I work. Dr Lennox, this is Mrs Benson, Cathy Benson—a friend of mine.'

'Are you her boss?' Cathy demanded.

Gabrielle could have sworn she saw his lips twitch slightly at the question. 'It's a fair description of the current situation,' he answered levelly.

Gabrielle ran her hand round the back of her neck, lifting the heavy swathe of hair away from her skin.

'Hardly,' she said wearily. 'It—it hasn't been actually resolved yet, Cathy. I don't know who I'll be working for.'

She saw the sardonic gleam in Shaun Lennox's eyes and waited resignedly for him to tell Cathy the truth of the situation.

'You're too modest, Mrs Warner, or is it just your love of secrecy again?' He turned to Cathy. 'But as you're such a close friend, Mrs Benson, I'm sure she won't mind me telling you that as from today she is the officially appointed photographer to our expedition to Ixtlacan.'

Gabrielle's own gasp of astonishment was drowned in Cathy's exuberant congratulations. She stared at him.

'When—when was this decision made?' Her voice trembled a little. 'Why was nothing said before?'

His brows rose. 'Dennis only finally made up his mind in the last twenty-four hours. You would have been told first thing this morning—if you'd been there. As it is, I've had to drive down here to take you back. I'm sorry to have to spoil your sightseeing, but an important briefing session has had to be delayed already so that you can be there.'

She flushed at the implied criticism. 'My days haven't been exactly full since I got to Merida, Dr Lennox.' She looked him straight in the eyes. 'I don't think I can be blamed if I take the opportunity to see some of the ruins I've dreamed about since I was a child.'

His smile was bland. 'Certainly not, Mrs Warner. But from now on I'm afraid you'll have to dream in your own time, not ours. And I promise you that you'll be far more concerned with realities in the next few weeks anyway.'

Gabrielle turned to Cathy, her smile forced. 'I'm sorry to break up the party like this, but it seems I have no choice. At least you'll be able to make your trip to the coast without having to worry about me.'

Cathy hesitated a moment, then she put her hand on Gabrielle's arm and drew her to one side.

'Are you sure you're O.K., honey?' Her voice was anxious. 'That was a nasty scare you had just now. You looked like a ghost. Would you rather we drove you back?'

'No—really.' Gabrielle tried to sound more reassuring than she felt. 'I'm fine. It's just that . . .'

'It's just that you don't want to hit it off with Dr High and Mighty Lennox,' Cathy supplied for her, and grinned. 'You had me going there for a moment. When he first showed up, I thought that he was . . .' She left the sentence unfinished and allowed her eyes to drift significantly to Gabrielle's wedding ring.

'Good God!' Gabrielle stared at her, aghast. 'What gave you that idea?'

'Just the way you reacted, honey,' Cathy's eyes flicked shrewdly over her. 'But if you're just good enemies, it's O.K. with me. It seems a waste, though. Gee, I'd better let you go. He's going to start grinding his teeth at any moment. I'll tell Jon what happened and we'll call you before we finally make for home.' A friendly hug and a smile and she was gone, leaving Gabrielle feeling oddly bereft, as if she had lost her last support in a hostile world.

'Are you finally ready, Mrs Warner?' Shaun Lennox walked over to her. 'I hope I haven't spoiled any private arrangements you may have had with your—friends.'

Gabrielle looked at him, puzzled by the faint ironic stress he had laid on the last word.

'Not really,' she said slowly. 'There was a vague idea of staying overnight somewhere at the coast and visiting Jean Lafitte's grave, but I'd already warned them not to include me.'

'Very predictable, tourist-like behaviour.' Now she knew she was not imagining the irony. 'How is it that you never mentioned this intimate friendship with the Bensons when you were acting like a waif and stray in Merida?'

'My friendship with Jon and Cathy is hardly of the intimate variety,' she retorted, her anger fired by his tone. 'I met them by chance at the Hotel Belen, and they were kind enough to invite me out with them. As it seemed to be my sole chance of seeing anything of the Yucatan before I was—dispatched back to England, I accepted. I didn't realise I was committing a criminal act, nor did I realise I was expected to hang around the Institute like a prisoner waiting for sentence.'

He looked down at her mockingly. 'Do I detect a note of petulance? You went to such lengths to convince me that you were a working girl that it didn't occur to me that you expected to be treated like a tourist as well.'

'I don't,' she cried indignantly.

'No?' He took her arm and began to walk her back along the sacred way. 'Perhaps I'll be more convinced when you can get rid of that look of girlish admiration for every pile of stones you see, and show me that you know a camera is intended for more than snapshots. Forget that you're a journalist, Mrs Warner, if that's indeed what you are. You're now a member of a scientific expedition, and you'll be judged by those standards. My standards.'

She fought back. 'If Professor Morgan thinks I'm capable . . .'

His eyes glinted lazily down at her. 'Dennis may have relented—against my advice—but you won't be able to use him as a court of appeal in the rain forest. He can't risk another bout of fever so soon, so he's staying behind at the Institute. I'm in charge of the expedition, and you will answer to me.'

Utter dismay silenced her. This was one development which had frankly never occurred to her. They were nearly back at the Castillo before she ventured to ask, 'But the copy to accompany the photographs? Professor Morgan was going to write it. I was told I had to work with him. If he's not going to be there . . .'

'Right again,' he said sardonically. 'Dennis has also passed on the responsibility for the words to go with your pictures. What's the matter, Mrs Warner? Don't you think we'll make a good team?'

'I wouldn't dare tell you what I think, Dr Lennox,' she said between her teeth.

'Nor I, Mrs Warner, believe me. I've parked the jeep over by the gatehouse. I don't see any sign of your friends. They don't seem to have wasted much time in making themselves scarce.'

The grimness in his tone did not escape her. She wrenched herself free of his touch and faced him.

'Do you have something against the Bensons, Dr Lennox?'

'Should I have?'

'It may be clever to answer one question with another, but it doesn't get us very far,' she said glacially. 'I'm getting very tired of these snide references you keep making. I don't know what the Bensons have done to arouse your disfavour—unless it's because they've been kind to me—but if there's something about them that I should know, I wish you'd tell me.'

He was silent for a moment. Then he said quietly, 'What have you heard about *esteleros*, Mrs Warner?'

Gabrielle stared back at him, her brain working quickly. 'Why, they're looters, aren't they? They steal things from sites that haven't been excavated properly and sell them abroad.'

'Right first time,' he applauded ironically. 'And no doubt a lady who has done her research as carefully as you have also knows that archaeologists derive most of their information about possible new sites in the forest from the *chicleros*, the men who go out collecting chewing gum from the trees. Sometimes they go along with us to act as guides and help carry equipment.'

'I'd heard that,' she admitted. 'But . . .'

'But what your background reading won't have told you,' he cut in smoothly, 'is that over the last few years

Institute expeditions have been invariably too late.'

She stared at him uncomprehendingly and he elaborated with a kind of weary patience, 'Someone had got there before us, Mrs Warner. The *esteleros*. I won't tell you what we found—temples desecrated, graves opened and robbed, stelae removed, glyphs defaced. They have to work fast, like all thieves in the night, so they can't take the care that we'd take. And they're completely ruthless too. If someone gets in their way—even if it's just a harmless *chiclero* who's happened to come blundering in—then they kill him. Things have got worse lately. Certain Communist guerrilla groups working against their own governments have realised the value of the sites as a source of revenue, so the *esteleros* are more highly organised than they have ever been.'

Gabrielle moistened her lips. 'I won't pretend I'm not interested by all this,' she said flatly. 'What I still don't understand, however, is what connection the Bensons have with all this.'

'Perhaps none. Perhaps they're what they seem to be—a pair of *norteamericanos* on a sightseeing tour of Mayan sites, who just happen to have taken pity on a lonely girl in a hotel lounge. But when the lonely girl is also married to an eminent member of the Institute and has come to Merida for the sole purpose of accompanying the next expedition—then, I must admit, my suspicions are aroused. I wonder if they'd have been as friendly to just *any* girl. I wonder too if just *any* girl would have responded quite so enthusiastically.'

'I think you're quite mad,' she said tightly. 'I refuse to believe that the Bensons are anything other than what they seem.'

'Your experience of life has taught you to be such an expert judge of character, has it?' He smiled mirthlessly at her sharp intake of breath.

She got into the jeep and sat, trembling slightly, as he

started the engine, her thoughts in utter turmoil. Was it possible there was a more sinister and devious motive for Jon and Cathy's friendliness than mere kindness of heart? She found it impossible to reconcile with the openness of their behaviour towards her. But Shaun Lennox's taunt about her knowledge of human nature had gone home. Her marriage was sufficient evidence of that, she thought, biting her lip.

'Have you spent an interesting day?' he inquired mockingly, after a lengthy silence. 'Has Chichen Itza lived up to all the demands of your imagination?'

'It was doing so,' she said in a low voice.

'Before I came along and spoiled it all?' he jeered.

She shrugged. 'You said it, Dr Lennox. I didn't. But I'm still not sure why you have come. I find it hard to swallow that my presence is suddenly so essential that you have to make a hundred-and-fifty-mile round trip to bring me back to the Institute—as if I was a runaway child or something.'

He sent her a swift look. 'Did you expect us not to be concerned about you? We're in some measure responsible for you.'

'I can look after myself,' she said raggedly.

'As you've so ably demonstrated in the past,' he shot at her.

'And I suppose you've never made a mistake in your life!' Her hands twisted together in her lap. 'You're very fortunate, Dr Lennox, to be able to walk through the world without doubts or uncertainties or the possibility of error.'

There was a brief silence before he spoke again, his voice harsh. 'Oh, I've had my share of problems, Mrs Warner. I can think of several quite serious mistakes I've been on the verge of making—quite recently.'

'Where do you count your—quarrel with my husband among all this?'

'Certainly not a mistake—more an inevitability.' Glancing sideways at him, she saw his profile become granite-hard, his mouth twisted slightly as if deprecating some unpalatable inner thought.

She moved her shoulders wearily. 'What was the quarrel about, or am I not allowed to ask?'

'You can ask. But I'm surprised you don't prefer to wait and hear James' version—if you haven't heard it already.'

'How could I possibly have done so?' Her green eyes widened as she stared at him, at the remote and implacable face half turned from her as he concentrated on the road ahead, and the cynical lines that had scored his mouth. 'I haven't seen James or heard from him since I arrived here, as you very well know.'

'I know, Mrs Warner? What do I know? Only what you choose to tell me, and how much dependence can we place on that, I wonder?'

'Now I know you're mad.' Her voice shook. 'What chance have I had—what possible opportunity has there been for James to communicate with me since I've been at the Institute? All my calls have been monitored by your switchboard—my every move has been questioned by someone . . .' The words tailed into silence as realisation came.

'Except for today,' he finished for her softly. 'Today when some obliging friends whisk you miles away where nothing you say or do can be questioned.'

'Is this why you came?' she whispered. 'Because you thought I was meeting James?' A bitter laugh escaped her. 'Then you've had a wasted journey, Dr Lennox. Even if James knows I'm in Yucatan, he hasn't made the slightest attempt to contact me since I arrived.' She hesitated. 'And if he did want to see me, he could always come to the Institute. He has as much right to be there as you have, Dr Lennox. He doesn't have to meet me in secret—in holes and corners. He's not a criminal. And I'm his wife.'

'That's one point I'm in no danger of forgetting.' His

voice was almost laconic, but there was another note in it that was not so easily identified.

'And why doesn't James come back to the Institute?' she ran on almost wildly. 'Is it you he's trying to avoid, Dr Lennox? Is it because of this quarrel? I think you're going to have to tell me what it was about. I have a right to know.'

'We won't argue about anyone's rights in the matter,' he said slowly. 'But if you insist on knowing—I suppose you could say James and I quarrelled about a woman.'

Speech deserted her. Then she laughed, hysterically. 'James—a woman? You don't—you can't expect me to believe that!'

He shrugged. 'Believe what you like. But basically it's the truth. What you need to question is the emphasis you yourself have placed on it, though, as you reminded me, you're James' wife and presumably know his—proclivities better than anyone else.'

Gabrielle bent her head, staring at the clenched fists lying in her lap. She was utterly confused, her mind wholly rejecting what she had been told. It was ludicrous, she told herself, but the thought brought its own bitter aftermath. Perhaps this was the explanation for James' coldness towards herself. Had he married her because he was miles away from the woman he really loved, and was lonely? Or had he required an English wife as protection against the demands of a more legal relationship with this other woman? A picture of James rose in her mind, and she considered it incredulously, trying to picture him with a Yucateca mistress—one of those petite, rather plump women with glossy raven's-wing hair she had seen on the streets of Merida. Someone whose warmth and passion might have charmed away that faint chill that she knew only too well, destroyed that academic precision, and even interfered with his obsession with the Maya. Gabrielle shivered in spite of the clammy heat that had invaded the whole of her body, trying to visualise such a woman back in London, occupying that museum of a flat. Was this why James had chosen her—because she was young, and too inexperienced with men and too shy to make inconvenient demands on him?

Shaun Lennox brought the jeep to a slithering halt at the side of the road, then he turned to her, taking her chin in hard, lean fingers before she could evade him, making her look at him.

'I'm beginning to wonder just how much you do know about the eminent Dr Warner,' he said quietly. 'Your reunion—when it occurs—should be an interesting one.'

'If it occurs,' she said stonily.

'Oh, you're bound to meet up with him eventually. After all, we all have a common goal—Ixtlacan. James is probably there, ahead of us.'

He released her and she moved almost imperceptibly away from him, along the bench seat. 'Is he still a member of the team, then, in spite of this—quarrel?'

'It's debatable whether James has ever been a—member of the team.' He produced a crumpled pack of cigarettes from his shirt pocket and offered them to her. She declined with a shake of her head. He lit one reflectively and blew out a lazy cloud of smoke. 'I've always regarded him as a loner—not easy to work with. At the same time, I'd have staked a considerable amount on his integrity.' He studied the glowing tip of his cigarette with narrowed eyes. 'That was one of the mistakes I referred to earlier.'

She shifted restlessly. 'It's hardly a matter of integrity. It's a personal matter—for James and myself.'

She said the words, amazed at the lack of feeling they engendered. She was a betrayed wife, and apparently a deserted one, and yet she felt ice-cold and empty inside. Where was the jealousy, the anger that should have been paramount in her emotions? All she had experienced so far was a feeling of sheer incredulity that did not involve her emotionally at all, and now this swelling, shaming sense of relief, like someone who sees a gleam of light appear in a tunnel that seemed endless.

'Do you love him?' The words were flung at her suddenly, shockingly, jolting her out of the confusion of her thoughts.

'I'm married to him.' It was hardly a reply, and it was born of shame rather than the truth.

'And you're a dutiful wife, of course.' He gave a harsh laugh, pitching his cigarette out on to the roadside, and restarting the engine with a jerk. 'And of course, every man is innocent until he's proved guilty. I hope, for your sake, Gabrielle, that James is innocent.'

Gabrielle slept badly that night, her dreams feverish and confused. She had half expected that Professor Morgan would interrogate her about her trip to Chichen Itza, but he made no reference to it at the evening conference, merely formally introducing her to the other expedition members, and explaining at some length the kind of feature that *Vision* envisaged. At the same time he made it clear that he would only be acting in an advisory capacity in the future, and that the expedition would be totally under Shaun Lennox's control. It was strange, Gabrielle thought, that some of the older men, who must have been more experienced than Shaun, did not show any signs of resentment. And she had to admit he handled his part of the conference well. The autocratic side of his nature seemed well under control. He spoke succinctly and even humorously, and gave due consideration to any other points that people raised. So he could be tactful and sensitive to other people's feelings—when he thought it mattered, she thought, and it was as if a knife twisted dully somewhere deep within her.

When she was finally alone in her room, she lay awake for a long time, staring into the darkness, trying to come to terms with the new perceptions that had come to her that day. She was sure now that she had never loved James, and felt it was as well that their relationship had never deepened into a true marriage. It was strange how the thought of his hands with their short, rather stubby fingers and fussily well-kept nails touching her body could make her shudder. The physical aspects of marriage had never preyed on her mind before. She had never imagined the demands a man's mouth and body against hers in the darkness might make.

She turned, burying her burning face almost convulsively in the cotton pillow. She had had to come halfway across the world to learn in one short, sharp lesson that desire was not governed by respect, liking or even familiarity as she had naïvely thought. None of these limitations applied in any way to what she felt about Shaun Lennox. And what did she feel about him? She closed her eyes so tightly that bright colour sparks danced crazily behind her lids. For a moment she let herself remember the way his mouth had moved on hers, the practised strength of his hands and the whole lean length of his muscular body—and stopped, ashamed and bewildered at the slow tide of warmth, the swift intimate ache of longing that these memories engendered. And her brain whispered, 'I hate him.'

It was an anti-climax the next morning to find that he had gone again. She only found out by accident. She had been assigned to work with Anna Lang, checking great lists of stores, including her own photographic and developing supplies which were due to be flown out to the base camp in the next few days. They worked mainly in silence. Anna was hardly the talkative type, and Gabrielle was too preoccupied with her own thoughts to initiate a conversation. At the same time she felt keyed up, listening with half an ear for the opening of the door behind her, the sound of Shaun's clipped resonant voice. But when eventually they were interrupted, it was Grace Morgan coming to tell them that coffee was ready. Gabrielle got up, stretching wearily, her restless night telling on her a little. As she reached the door, she heard Anna say quietly, 'When will Shaun get back from Villahermosa?'

She walked to the big sitting room where most of the other expedition members were already sprawled on the wide sofas and armchairs and helped herself to coffee in silence. She was being ridiculous, she told herself, walking across to the patio doors and staring out into the sunshine-filled courtyard with unseeing eyes. There was no other way to describe the sudden leap her heart had given when she heard his name. Had it been excitement or panic? Whatever it had been, she wanted no part of it. She was behaving like an adolescent, and the situation that faced her called for maturity. She had to forget about everything except that she had a job to do, a job that called on her to work closely with him. It would not be the last time she would have to work with someone she actively disliked, she thought, stifling any other interpretation of the swift pang she had felt on knowing he was no longer at the Institute.

It was stupid too to feel slighted because she was so obviously the only person at the Institute who had no idea that he had gone on another trip. It made her still feel an outsider, that although she was now to all intents and purposes part of the team, there was still a side to the work that was being kept from her. Or was she just letting the emotional disturbance she felt give colour to her imagination? Everyone had been kind, without being over-effusive, and heaven knew she didn't expect special treatment. There was just something ... She gave a brief sigh and sipped at her coffee, appreciating its strong, crisp flavour.

Over the next few days, when she had time to think at all, Gabrielle sometimes wondered how she had ever found the atmosphere at the Institute restful. The air of excitement that had been slowly building up could no longer be described as subdued. Most of the stores had gone and the advance party who were to be responsible for establishing the base camp had also left. Even Anna Lang shook off some of her quiet imperturbability, and joked with some of the volatile French archaeologists about the extent of the discoveries it was hoped to make.

She seemed so much more approachable that Gabrielle decided to ask her about their exact destination. She felt rather foolish having to ask such a basic question, almost on the point of setting out, but it seemed clear that everyone else assumed she knew already.

Anna seemed surprised at her ignorance, but she readily fetched a map and spread it over the big table in the Institute library.

'We fly first to Yaxchilan. There's an air strip there,' she said, pointing. 'Then we go by boat up the Rio Usamacinta to the base camp.'

'But I thought the excavations were at Yaxchilan.'

'Oh, no.' Anna shook her head decisively. 'The Mexican government are determined to maintain some areas in as —unspoiled a condition as possible. They've never allowed anything but the minimum of work at Yaxchilan. No, this is a trip into unknown territory for most of us.'

It was a slightly nerve-racking thought, but Gabrielle could catch some of the older woman's excitement at the prospect.

'Then where exactly is Ixtlacan?' she asked.

Anna shrugged a little. 'None of us know the exact location,' she said rather vaguely. 'It's better that way. We rely on the *chicleros* who made the original discovery to take us there. All I've heard Shaun say is that the site lies between two of the tributaries that feed the Usamacinta. The Mayans say one of the tributaries is cursed—*torcido* —and maybe this is why not much exploration has gone on in the region. On the other hand, people could simply have stumbled past the site without even knowing it was there.'

'It would be pretty hard to miss, surely.' Gabrielle stared at her.

Anna smiled. 'Not really. You've never been in the rain forest and you don't know what it can do. It's the most successful form of camouflage there is. You can walk within inches of a pyramid and think it was simply a vine-covered hillock. It's like a fierce, green curtain that dares you to probe behind it, and sometimes, if you dare lift the curtain, the rewards can be—infinite.'

'Do you think the rewards will be infinite at Ixtlacan?'

'Who knows?' Anna shrugged slightly. It was as if she had withdrawn back into her shell, slightly ashamed of the feeling she had allowed herself to show for the cruel, beautiful world she had made her life. 'The *chicleros* seemed very excited. If only we're not too late ...' She cut herself off abruptly, as if she had said too much.

'You mean the *estoleros*?' Gabrielle asked.

'Er—yes.' Anna's manner seemed oddly hesitant, suddenly. 'They're a scourge,' she added with real bitterness.

'Dr Lennox was telling me about them.' Gabrielle hated herself for the constraint that entered her voice when she mentioned his name. She hoped Anna had not noticed.

'Shaun? Yes, he would. He hates them more than anybody. He feels this Mayan heritage has been entrusted to us, and that we still have so much to learn about them. We still haven't grasped more than the barest essentials about their mathematical and scientific knowledge, and this is why it's so important for these sites to remain undisturbed. Yet these vultures come down and destroy the sites before any serious investigation can begin, selling the artefacts off to museums and collectors who should know better, scattering priceless evidence across the world so that it can never be pieced together again.' She gave a slight laugh. 'Goodness, I am getting carried away! I must apologise, Mrs Warner.'

'There's no need,' Gabrielle said eagerly. 'I feel the same as you do.' She looked down at the map again, not noticing the odd, sideways glance Anna gave her as if she was puzzled about something.

'The Rio Torcido,' she said quietly, and shivered a little. 'I—I wonder if it really is cursed.'

'I hope not.' Anna rolled up the map with a decisive gesture. 'I think the Institute has had all the bad luck it can cope with in recent months.'

Gabrielle nodded, not fully understanding. She wondered if James' disappearance was included in this bad luck by his colleagues. It seemed curious that none of them ever discussed it with her, or voiced any theories about where he was. Perhaps they were all waiting for her to make the first move, she thought. But all the same it was an uncomfortable sensation, suggesting in a way that as far as the Institute was concerned, James had never existed. Out of curiosity one day, she had tried the handle of the room she had visited the first time she had come to the Institute, but his card was missing from the door, and the room was locked. Sometimes at dinner, when the conversation was ranging as it always did over a variety of general topics, Gabrielle had a sudden longing to stand up and shriek, 'Will someone please tell me what's going on?' But at the last minute her courage always deserted her. They would probably think she had gone mad, she told herself. And even if her suspicions were justified, and there were things being kept from her, such an outburst would only succeed in making them close their ranks against her.

'I think,' Grace Morgan announced buoyantly at breakfast one morning, 'that we'll have a party for you all before you go.'

Pierre Rosteau looked at her, his dark face crinkling into a rueful smile. 'Maybe it's a good idea, *hein*? To celebrate now in case there is—nothing to celebrate when we return.'

For a second the atmosphere was electric and Gabrielle knew with a sudden stirring of intuition that this was as close as she had ever got to finding an answer for the things that puzzled at the Institute, then someone laughed too loudly, and the moment went, and everyone started talking about the party, arguing lightheartedly about the food and drink and offering records and tapes for music.

In spite of her private anxieties, Gabrielle's spirits lifted at the thought of a party. She knew what she would wear. On one of her infrequent shopping trips in Merida, she had bought herself an *ipil* in exquisitely woven white linen, the low neck and wide hem heavily encrusted with green and gold embroidery. And she had included in her luggage as an afterthought a pair of green trousers, silken and slightly flared, which would provide the perfect accompaniment, she thought, cool and not too elaborate.

Because of the warmth of the evening, the tables of food had been set out in the courtyard, Gabrielle discovered when she came downstairs. A score of delicious odours were scenting the air and she sniffed appreciatively as she stepped through the patio doors on to the terrace. In one corner, a trio of local musicians were beamingly playing guitars in swinging, rhythmic cadences that spoke of an older culture than the Spanish courtyard in which they stood. Imperceptibly her spirits lifted.

'Have a drink?' Anna Lang, tall and remote in her dark, rather severely cut dress, turned to her with a faint smile. 'We have *tepache* if you think your head can stand it, or if you prefer something unfermented, I can recommend *tamarindo*. Apart from that there's beer on ice, and the usual spirits.'

Gabrielle accepted a *tamarindo* and took a tentative sip.

It was unexpectedly sour for a fruit drink, but as her palate accustomed itself, she found it pleasant and refreshing. Glass in hand, she moved back into the shadows, content to remain an onlooker. Several couples were already dancing energetically, and Pierre Rosteau, jigging contentedly with his small dark-haired wife, lifted a hand in acknowledgement as he spied her there. Seeing them all there and listening to the laughter and chatter, Gabrielle thought it was impossible that there could be the undercurrents she suspected. They must all be figments of her own overheated imagination. Perhaps no one talked about James to her because they were embarrassed. She was, after all, in the age-old position of the wife who was the last one to know of her husband's infidelity. It was a humiliating situation, but no more of a humiliation than the rest of her life had been with James, she thought bitterly. At least this lapse proved that he could be human in his reactions—something she had begun to doubt.

She smiled lightly as the music switched to a rapid waltz tempo, and she saw Professor Morgan and his wife take to the floor. The Professor still looked tired—the aftermath, Gabrielle supposed, of his recent bout of fever—but he was smiling lightheartedly enough and if he had private worries, he was keeping them to himself.

She started slightly when a tentative voice at her elbow said, '*Señora?*' Looking round, she saw Rosita who worked in the Institute office, accompanied by a dark, short young man whom Gabrielle guessed was her *novio*. She liked Rosita, who seemed always smiling and performed her office duties with an air of willingness, in marked contrast to Isabella who behaved usually as if she was bestowing a favour. And she was grateful to her for helping over the misunderstanding at the Hernandez Bar. Something told her that if it had been Isabella instead, she could well have been left to her plight. So she was glad to talk to Rosita and her rather solemn Manuel in her halting Spanish, and they achieved a fair level of understanding. She soon discovered that neither of them could comprehend her desire to accompany the expedition to Ixtlacan, and Manuel seemed particularly disapproving even though Gabrielle guessed Rosita was explaining to him in a torrent of soft-voiced Spanish that the *señora* hoped to be reunited there with her husband. His whole dour expression indicated that a dutiful wife would remain in Merida and wait for her husband to come to her.

'Hay peligro, señora,' he kept repeating firmly, and Gabrielle, mentally reviewing her scanty Spanish, realised with a sinking heart that he was telling her that there was danger. But she knew that already, didn't she? she told herself stoutly. She tried to joke Manuel out of his seriousness, asking him the nature of the danger. Was if from snakes—or from animals perhaps? Or even from the old gods—angry that strangers were intruding on their domain? But immediately she knew she had said the wrong thing, and that in spite of centuries of conventional religion, the people of the Yucatan still took the influence of the ancient gods very seriously.

Gabrielle could only understand one word in a dozen of Manuel's reply, and Rosita, her brow puckered in distress, had too limited a knowledge of English to help to translate. But one word Gabrielle did recognise, and again she felt chilled. It was the word Anna Lang had used about the river they were to explore—*'torcido'*. Accursed.

She swung on Rosita. *'Lo, siento, no comprendo,'* she began apologetically, when a very different voice cut in.

'He's telling you, Mrs Warner, that those who approach the old gods without respect to plunder their treasures will be punished.'

She had been so lost in the difficulties of her conversation with Rosita and Manuel that she entirely failed to notice Shaun Lennox's arrival. In fact she'd had no inkling from anyone that he intended to be at the party. Now he stood a few feet away from the little group, lithe and attractive in dark, close-fitting pants and a snowy *guayabera*, its pleated neckline open almost to his waist, revealing a broad expanse of darkly tanned chest. Seeing him in the traditional shirt worn by most Yucatecos, Gabrielle immediately felt self-conscious about her own choice of costume, and wished she had worn something definitely European. He looked her up and down, and grinned a little mockingly as if he could read her thoughts.

She swallowed, her throat feeling suddenly dry and husky.

'Then perhaps you could explain to Manuel for me, Dr Lennox, that I have no intention of going to—plunder. That all I want is to take some pictures.'

'I'll try, Mrs Warner,' he murmured. 'But I doubt if I'll be able to do justice to that note of passionate sincerity of yours. You almost have me convinced.'

She stood, her hands clenched into tight balls of tension, while he made his explanation to Manuel and Rosita, all her pleasure in the evening destroyed. He was back, her adversary, and she supposed dully these fencing matches of theirs would have to continue until he chose to lower his blade. It never occurred to her to try and take the offensive away from him. She wondered, somewhat hopelessly, what it would be like to be on terms of easy intimacy and friendship with him, like Anna Lang who wandered up, calling a greeting, or Pierre Rosteau or Craig Lesley, one of the Americans, who gathered round him, clapping him on the shoulder and teasing him about his absence in Villahermosa. He was still the expedition leader, but they all seemed to find it possible to meet him on equal terms. Yet his attitude towards herself was strangely ambivalent. At one moment he seemed to regard her as if she was some brainless sex object, but at the next, he was holding her at arms' length, treating her with a kind of wary contempt. Both attitudes were completely unfair, she thought hotly, but at the same time she had not the least idea what, if anything, she could do to alter them, or even to find a valid explanation for them. It was like being condemned without a trial, she thought.

'Saying a few prayers as insurance, Mrs Warner?'

She came back to reality with a start, to find that the others had all moved off, leaving them alone together.

'Don't look so panic-stricken,' he advised softly. 'I'm only going to ask you to dance. Is that such a hardship?'

She swallowed, knowing it was the last thing in the world that she wanted, to have to go publicly into his arms, and feel the warm strength of his body against hers.

But what choice did she have? If she made an excuse, pleaded tiredness or a headache, she knew he would not believe her, and she could imagine only too well what his caustic tongue would make of the situation, so she let him take her hand and draw her out of the shadows into the middle of the courtyard, brilliant under its gay, hanging lamps. And, as if to spite her, the tempo changed yet again, becoming slow and almost dreamy, giving him every reason to draw her close against him. Her hands went up instinctively to hold him off, only to encounter his bare skin.

'What's the matter?' His arms linked around her waist tightened as he felt her involuntary recoil. His tone hardened. 'I'm not diseased, Gabrielle, nor am I untouchable.'

'I'm sorry,' she said tightly. 'I'm just not used to—dancing like this.'

His lip curled. 'For a married woman, you seem to have led a remarkably sheltered life.'

She did not meet his gaze, thankful that he would never appreciate the true irony of that remark.

'So tomorrow, Gabrielle, all your dreams come true.'

'I don't think I have many dreams left,' she said in a low voice.

'And for that I'm responsible, I suppose. Maybe you

should be grateful to me. Illusions only bring very temporary comfort, you know.'

She had a bleak desire to tell him that any kind of comfort would be welcome, but she bit her lip. His pity would be unbearable.

'You're not very talkative,' he observed after a moment or two. 'Don't you want to know what I've been doing in Villahermosa?'

She looked up at him, forcing herself to speak steadily. 'I can't imagine that it's any business of mine, Dr Lennox.'

'Every other member of this expedition addresses me as Shaun,' he said. 'Don't you think it's going to cause comment if you continue to behave with this absurd formality?'

She tilted her chin a little. 'Are you proposing a truce—Dr Lennox?'

His dark brows drew together. 'I'd hardly say that—merely suggesting that in the sort of inter-dependence we shall all be experiencing shortly, there's no room for personalities or temperaments.'

'I can promise you that you'll have no cause for complaint where I'm concerned. In fact, I don't think there'll be much need for us to have any personal contact at all.'

'You little bitch,' he said softly. 'Haven't you forgotten something—that you're relying on me to supply the text to go with your pictures?'

Gabrielle had forgotten, and mentally she kicked herself.

'And while we're making promises,' his voice dropped another tone, 'here's one for you. That you'll never forget any—personal contact—that there is between us for as long as you live. Whether or not you have cause for complaint remains to be seen.'

His arms tightened round her so unbearably, she thought her spine would snap under the pressure, but she stared up at him defiantly, refusing to reveal any of the physical or emotional discomfort she was feeling. The music came to a halt in a triumphant swirl of chords, and she was released, feeling half-faintly that she would bear the pressure marks of his fingers for the rest of her life.

His voice was too light as he said, 'Thank you, my dear Mrs Warner. That was delightful.'

His smile skimmed over her, widening slightly as he took in the shadowy lift of her breasts under the fine linen of her *ipil*, and the slender curves of her hips and thighs in the clinging trousers.

And as the laughter and chatter swelled up around them, she heard in a daze, his whisper meant for her ears alone. 'And that, Gabrielle, is just for starters.'

CHAPTER FIVE

GABRIELLE woke with a start and lay for a minute, trying to get her bearings. From the adjoining camp bed, she could hear Anna's gentle, rhythmic breathing and she relaxed again almost imperceptibly. The sound that had roused her initially came again—a strident chilly scream descending to a throbbing moan.

Howler monkeys, she thought sleepily, no longer alarmed on her third night in the rain forest by the uncanny noise they made. Through the slatted windows of the prefabricated hut they were occupying, she could see that the sun was already up, and she stretched lazily inside the sheltering mosquito netting, welcoming the advent of another day.

In spite of everything, she was here, she thought drowsily, and she had no regrets. The only disturbing factor for James' continuing absence. She had really begun to believe as the helicopter descended towards the landing strip at the base camp that he was there among the crowd of tiny figures below who had assembled to watch the rest of the party arrive, and in spite of this initial disappointment she had remained on edge for the rest of the evening, expecting him to suddenly appear. But there had been no sign of him, and although she had desperately wanted to ask someone if they had any idea of his present whereabouts, she had been unsure whom to approach. The silence that had prevailed in Merida seemed to exist here as well, she recognised uneasily.

The obvious person to ask was, of course, Shaun Lennox, but under the circumstances, this was impossible. She had managed to keep well out of his way during these first days at the camp. The more she thought about their last encounter, and it was constantly on her mind, the more perplexing it became. Why had he mentioned his trip to Villahermosa so pointedly? Had he been seeking news of James? Even if it was true, it was too late now for her to follow it up. Common sense dictated that she should avoid him as much as possible. She moved restlessly, hitching her sleeping bag over her shoulder. The best thing she could do, she had decided, was to concentrate all her energies on the completion of the assignment that had brought her here, and relegate her personal problems to the back of her mind as far as possible.

She rolled over slightly and looked across at Anna, but the older woman was still sleeping the sleep of the just. Long experience had probably inured her to the alarms and discomforts of primitive surroundings, Gabrielle supposed wryly. And yet by camp standards, their facilities were almost luxurious. Being women, she had soon learned, earned them certain privileges, the privacy of a small hut to sleep in, for one thing. Most of the party slept in the open in jungle hammocks, swathed in netting and slung among the trees beneath palm-thatched roofs. They had also been accorded certain bathing times in the nearby river, and the men scrupulously kept to the camp during these times. Gabrielle had been reluctant to trust herself in the brown-looking water at first. Her flesh crawled to think what might be lurking beneath the placid surface, but Anna had laughed at her apprehensions, warning her frankly that the specially purified water had to be kept for drinking and cooking, and advising her to take full advantage of the river while she could.

One end of the long hut which the archaeologists would be using to clean, examine and classify their finds had been turned into a small dark room, powered by one of the small portable generators in use at the site. The facilities might be basic, Gabrielle thought, but they were perfectly adequate for black and white work. She had already begun work, photographing the layout of the camp and its personnel. She had even taken some pictures of the surrounding area, her imagination caught by the towering trees shrouded by twisting lianas, but after a stern warning from Pierre Rosteau, she had been careful not to stray too far towards the encircling jungle, slightly abashed when he had shown her the unmistakable signs of jaguar tracks only yards from their clearing.

She unzipped her sleeping bag and unhitched the netting with care. Leaning out of bed, she found her shoes and shook them out to ensure they had attracted no unexpected inhabitants during the night. She grimaced as she remembered the first spider which had fallen from the roof and landed in front of her on the table in the exhibits hut. It had been black and almost as large as the palm of her hand, and she had frozen with fear just looking at it. Fortunately Anna had come in just then and scared it away, agreeing that yes, it probably was a tarantula, but not particularly dangerous, and anyway far more frightened of Gabrielle than she was of it—a proposition that Gabrielle doubted.

Fortunately, the only snake she had encountered so far had been a very dead one—a coral snake hacked in two by someone's machete.

'Good riddance,' Craig Lesley had remarked laconically, observing the two motionless halves, and no one had disagreed with him.

Moving as quietly as possible, Gabrielle collected her towel and sponge bag and huddled on the minimum clothing which was all the heat and damp of her surroundings permitted. It wasn't the allotted bathing time yet, but it was too early for anyone else in the camp to be stirring, she told herself. She would have the unaccustomed luxury of a bathe in private and be able to make an early start on her work. The two *chicleros* whose discoveries deep in the jungle had led to the expedition being mounted in the first place had arrived late the previous night, and Gabrielle wanted to get some shots of them before they were required for other purposes. So far she had managed to keep her work fairly unobtrusive, and she wanted it to stay that way.

She let herself carefully out of the hut and waved at the two startled Mayan cooks, who were the only other people about, busily preparing *tortillas* for the day ahead. In many ways, the camp had a sort of weird civilisation, she thought, looking critically about her at the tall water tanks on stilts, the ranks of huts raised on blocks away from the prevailing damp of the ground, and the blackened areas around the cooking fires. The next stage, she knew soberly, was going to be much harder. They would be plunging into the unknown, carrying most of their supplies on their backs, and travelling as far as they could by boat, using their legs at other times. Gabrielle hoped apprehensively that hers would hold out. Walking had never been one of her pastimes and her confidence had suffered a further jolt at Anna's casual references to trips down the Pennine Way on foot as well as several crossings of the famous Lyke Wake Walk in North Yorkshire.

Gabrielle was finding it harder than she had ever imagined to maintain her energy. No matter how careful she was, by midday she felt limp and exhausted. The humidity seemed to seep into the very fibre of her being, sapping her willpower along with her physical strength, and dampening her hair, clothes and skin.

But any discomfort had seemed bearable suddenly the previous night when someone had put a piece of stone in her hand, and she had been able to trace with her own finger the intricate, man-made carvings it bore. All her reading and dreaming took on a new reality. Centuries fell away and history became tangible as she felt the surge of excitement that accompanies any new discovery.

Even Anna had seemed unwontedly exhilarated as they prepared for bed, explaining that from what she had managed to decipher from the pieces of broken glyph that Pablo and Francisco had brought, it seemed likely that the ruins they had found were part of a shrine to the moon goddess Ixchel.

'Most of the worship of the goddess was confined to the island of Cozumél—miles from here,' Anna said. 'I don't think I've come across many inland shrines to her. Yet there's no reason why she shouldn't have been more widely worshipped. She was patroness of medicine and the arts, as well as being married to the sun god.'

Gabrielle listened entranced. She was fully aware of the importance of sun-worship in the pre-conquest cultures of central and southern America, but had never considered that the moon might also have a part to play in these rituals. And yet, she supposed, it was only logical that the flamboyantly male sun should need a female counterpart—cool, chilly and mysterious. She checked herself inwardly, knowing that she was being fanciful. But surely this was an occasion when dream and fancy could go hand in hand with science, she thought. Where myth and legend could blend with the solid presence of the pyramids and stelae.

Some of the same feeling of wonder remained with her as she trod warily down the narrow track leading to the river, her eyes sharpened for tell-tale tracks and avoiding clumps of vegetation where a snake might be coiled. Above her head, birds chattered in the twining thicket of branches, vines and leaves which allowed only fleeting glimpses of the sky and sun.

When she reached the river, she stood for a few moments looking around her, absorbing the utter peace of the scene. Somewhere near at hand monkeys were babbling excitedly, and a great black and white bird rose from a tree and flew away, its wings flapping like muted pistol shots.

It was idyllic, she thought wryly, and it would be so easy to ignore the inherent dangers and revel in its sheer primitive appeal.

She slipped out of her clothes, hanging them on a conveniently jutting branch, then slid without a splash into the cool water, ducking her head underneath it while she used the tiny sachet of shampoo she had brought. The water felt delicious on her skin and hair and she swam lazily, letting her hands slip over the rounded stones on the river bed. It's like Eden, she told herself, and giggled aloud at the idea of herself as Eve. But her smile faded slightly as she remembered Eden had also included an Adam ... She closed her mind firmly to the fantasies that line of thinking could engender and swam towards the bank. She would have to get back. The whole camp would be awake by now and she might be missed. She scrambled up on to the bank and, retrieving her towel, began to dry herself.

She registered the splash almost incuriously, telling herself it was a dead branch. Certainly it wasn't loud enough to be a large animal, human or otherwise. She turned, half idly, to check her theory and felt the scream coming, bubbling up out of her throat as she saw the weird dragon face, horned and malevolent, watching her from the water. Then she ran blindly, oblivious of the vines and creepers which entangled her bare, flying feet, the slipping towel or the droplets from her soaking hair which mingled with the frightened tears on her face.

'Dear God!' Her headlong flight was blocked suddenly. Hard hands gripped her shoulders, forcing her to stillness. 'What in the name of hell are you doing away from the camp—alone? Why were you screaming? What's happened? Answer me, damn you!'

She looked up at Shaun Lennox, his eyes dark and brilliant with anger. The flood of relief that filled at the sight of him was incomprehensible—and a little frightening—but it was real.

'I was bathing.' She choked out the words.

'I can see that,' he said coldly, and for the first time she realised how she must look, naked except for a totally inadequate and very damp towel. And for him of all men to find her like this, she thought wildly, vainly trying to clutch the towel around her as a wave of heat swept over her body.

His anger showed no sign of moderation. 'I thought I'd laid down times when you and Anna were to bathe. I made it clear everyone else was to keep away. Has someone dared . . .?'

'No—oh, no. There was—something in the water. A—a dragon.' Her voice tailed away, knowing how ridiculous her story sounded.

'A dragon!' The contempt in his voice was withering. 'Show me this—dragon, and I'll slay it for you—unless you'd prefer to complete your striptease.'

'My clothes are down by the river,' she mumbled, her eyes fixed on the ground, her face crimson.

He left her to make her own way, striding on ahead with obvious impatience. Gabrielle paused to adjust the towel more discreetly, anchoring it round her sarong-wise. When she reached the river, he was standing staring at the unbroken surface of the water.

'But there was something——' she began almost desperately, as she came up beside him. He turned to her swiftly, silencing her with a finger to his lips. A few seconds later there was another louder splash and Gabrielle cried out involuntarily at the sight of the long lizard body cutting through the water.

'That's your dragon,' Shaun said drily. 'An iguana. It's big, I grant you, and it's not pretty, but it's relatively harmless—unless your small boat happens to be underneath it when it performs its diving act.'

'It looked like a dinosaur.' Her heartbeat was steadying now, and she was ready to die of shame at her own absurdity.

'I suppose so. Did you think you'd stumbled on another Lost World?' He turned and smiled at her, and for the first time he seemed genuinely amused, his laughter with her and not at her. 'Poor dragon,' he said after a moment. 'He probably thought you were just a different brand of iguana and decided to join you. Who can blame him?'

She was suddenly uneasy again, aware of the solitude and her own near-nudity. She backed away from him a little, holding on to the towel with one hand and reaching up to the branch for her shirt and jeans with the other.

'Thank you, Dr Lennox,' she said primly. 'I—I'll get dressed now, I think.'

'I'm not stopping you.' He rested his hands on his hips and stood watching her. His blue eyes had lost that dark and stormy look, and seemed almost to be dancing, she thought distractedly.

'I can't—not with you here.' She tried for a note of sweet reason, but couldn't subdue the shake in her voice. She knew too that she was blushing and wished that the ground would open and swallow her.

His brows rose mockingly. 'It was precisely to avoid this kind of situation that I told you and Anna to bathe together at set times. You chose to disregard my dictum, so you can pay the penalty.' His smile was wicked suddenly. 'There can be worse things than dragons, fair maiden. You don't mind if I call you that? Fair matron doesn't sound right at all.'

He started towards her and, panic-stricken, she put out a hand to ward him off.

'Shaun,' she said breathlessly, and she knew the breathlessness was not caused by fear but by another emotion just as old and equally basic.

He paused. 'You called me by my name. Is it a token concession, or have you decided that it's foolish to be formal any longer now you've been naked in my arms?'

'I—I wasn't naked,' she said between dry lips.

His smile widened. 'From where I was . . .' he said gently. Around them the forest stirred and whispered. Creatures moved, and a bird cried with harsh stridency. But the only sound Gabrielle heard was the remorseless pounding of her own heart. He came towards her, and the mockery was stilled, and the laughter was dead.

'It was good, Gabrielle.' His voice was quiet. 'I want it again. You—in my arms—like that.'

His hands were gentle on her, his thumbs caressing her jawline, the smooth line of her throat and the curves at its base. They found the bareness of her shoulders and traced a lingering path across the partly-revealed curves of her breasts. She felt the towel slip away, down below her waist, and all the instincts of a lifetime screamed at her to cover herself with her hands. But instead she stood in silence, her hands unresistingly at her sides, while he looked at her. Then he reached for her, his hands tangling fiercely in the damp brightness of her hair as he lifted her face to his mouth.

Her lips parted almost eagerly beneath his. Her response was shy at first, but, after a moment or two, invested with a growing awareness of her own sensuality. She thought with a sense of wonder, 'I want him,' and knew that it was no new thing that she acknowledged but something inevitable that she had fought against since the first time she had seen him in that hotel in Merida.

His hands discovered the soft swell of her breasts and the hardening of her nipples, before exploring her delicate rib cage and the sweet curves of her waist and abdomen. They reached the towel, still clinging damply to her hips, and he paused fractionally, his eyes questioning the sudden shyness in hers as he began to loosen the folds of material.

He drew a breath sharply. 'Gabrielle . . .'

Her name floated back like an echo from the trees. Anna's voice, questioning and alarmed.

'Gabrielle! Where are you? Are you all right?'

She heard him curse, swiftly and softly under his breath. Then he called back.

'It's O.K., Anna, I've found her. She's had a bit of a scare.'

His hands slackened and fell away from her. Silently he reached up to the branch and lifted down her clothes, holding them out to her.

'You'd better put them on,' he advised briefly, and turned away. Gabrielle was trembling so much that she could hardly pull up the zip on her jeans or force the buttons of her shirt through the appropriate holes. She knew she would never be able to fix her belt through the loops on her jeans, so she carried it over her arm.

When she was dressed, she stood quite still, like a child waiting to be told what to do next. Eventually he turned and looked at her. The lover who had held her with such passionate demand only minutes before and the man who now confronted her were strangers. His face was hard and bleak, his eyes like chips of ice.

'I owe you an apology.' His voice was clipped. 'I forgot—I keep forgetting—that you're married. That you aren't—free to choose what you want to do. I'm sorry. It won't happen again.'

'What if I told you I was free—free to make any choice I wanted?' She looked at him. 'What then?'

'It wouldn't make a ha'porth of difference,' he said, his tone cold and flat. 'You're still Warner's wife. Your choice has been made.'

'Shaun, listen.' She made herself walk towards him, putting her hand out almost timidly. 'You—you don't understand . . .'

He stepped back from her, his slanting brows drawn together in a thunderous frown.

'Isn't it usually the erring male who complains of being misunderstood?' The bitter mockery she detested was back in his voice. 'Get back to camp, Gabrielle. One man has sacrificed his integrity for you already. I won't add my name to the list.'

He turned away, thrusting his hands roughly into his pockets, walking ahead of her up the path back to camp.

She followed more slowly, aching with a mixture of sensations and emotions, shame, hurt pride, misery and unsatisfied desire all wreaking havoc within her.

'Shaun.'

He turned and looked back at her. She had wanted to ask him what he had been about to say when Anna called, but the words wouldn't come. Instead, she heard herself say, 'Who was the woman you quarrelled over with James?'

He looked at her, a long hard look which seemed not just to strip the clothes from her body, but the flesh from the slender bones beneath.

'It was you, Gabrielle,' he said, and walked away.

She was amazed how pride, however damaged, could come to the rescue. It enabled her to get back to camp, and accept Anna's rather anxious reproaches with an appearance of contrition. She was even able to turn the incident with the iguana into an amusing adventure, touching with incredible lightness on Shaun's role as a knight errant.

'Oh, they are dreadful-looking things.' Anna was sympathetic. 'You're looking very white. Perhaps you'd better lie down for a while.'

'Oh, no!' Gabrielle was horrified. She wanted no suggestion that she wasn't up to the trip, unable to take these everyday alarms in her stride. Some intuition told her that even at this late stage she could find herself aboard one of the supply helicopters, on her way back to Merida. Apart from anything else, she would now be an embarrassment to Shaun, she thought unhappily. He would be only too glad of an excuse to get rid of her.

'I think I can stand one major shock before breakfast,' she went on with an assumption of gaiety.

'As long as that's all.' Anna frowned slightly, then said in a low voice, 'I know you're under a strain, Gabrielle, but so are we all. Try and relax more, if you can. Things will work out somehow, you'll see.'

She gave Gabrielle's arm a quick, awkward squeeze as if she was unused to such demonstrations and went out of the hut. Gabrielle sank down on the edge of the bed, feeling that her legs would no longer support her. What did Anna mean? she wondered helplessly. Was she referring to a relationship between Shaun and herself? A slow knife twisted painfully within her at the idea.

She had never felt so totally confused in her life. Her mind was still reeling from Shaun's answer to her question. How could James and he have quarrelled over her? He'd had no idea she had any connection with James until she told him so herself. She gave a weary sigh and buried her face in her hands. She seemed confronted with riddles at every turn, riddles to which everyone seemed to have the answer but herself.

At breakfast, eaten at a large trestle table set away from the smoke of the cooking fires, she had to endure some good-natured teasing from Pierre and Craig, but she accepted it in good part, knowing resignedly that the incident was likely to become part of camp history. She could only be thankful that no one knew of the devastating aftermath to the story. It was a relief too in some ways that Shaun did not appear at breakfast. By the time she had to face him again, she might have had time to rebuild the barrier around her emotions, re-kindle even the fires of the antagonism she had made herself feel for him.

She began work immediately the meal was over. Neither Pablo nor Francisco were averse to having themselves photographed with their finds. Indeed they were almost embarrassingly eager, and Gabrielle found to her dismay that they were determined to pose for the camera, smiling widely. Her few Spanish phrases seemed woefully inadequate to explain to them that was not what she intended—that she wanted to photograph them studying the pieces of stone, not staring with anticipation at the lens. The more halting her explanations became, the wider and more obliging their smiles. Pablo even removed his wide-brimmed hat and combed his hair more becomingly with a tiny piece of broken comb that he produced from somewhere on his person.

She was becoming almost desperate when Shaun said levelly behind her, 'Having trouble?'

She turned to him gratefully, forgetting that she had been dreading having to meet him again.

'Yes—I can't explain what I want them to do. They will keep looking at me, and not at the glyphs. I want them to forget I'm here—that the camera and I even exist. I want them to start talking about the glyphs and about Ixtlacan. When people talk they forget to be self-conscious and you get much more natural-looking shots.'

He studied her for a moment with raised brows, then turned to the two *chicleros*, apparently translating her remarks into swift Spanish. She waited rather anxiously for their reaction, but was not prepared for them both to break into shouts of uproarious laughter. Pablo recovered first, and began jabbering away in return, his hands gesturing in a way that aroused Gabrielle's suspicions.

'What's he saying?' she asked, the colour rising in her face.

Shaun gave her a dry look. 'I assume you don't want a literal translation. He's suggesting that no red-blooded man could ever forget you were present.'

'Oh.' She was blushing hotly now. 'Well, will they do as I ask?'

'Oh, yes.' He grinned suddenly. 'And more. I imagine whatever you suggested would meet with their whole-hearted co-operation.'

'I see.' She avoided his glance, pretending to make some minute adjustment to her camera setting. 'It's—it's just as well I have a competent interpreter, or I could be in all kinds of trouble.'

'Don't say you weren't warned.' There was a certain

grimness in his tone. She watched him stride away with a feeling of bleakness. She'd had a childish wish that he would stay and watch her at work, so that he could see for himself that she knew what she was doing and that she was as much a professional in her way as he was in his. It was uncomfortable feeling that she was included on the expedition on sufferance, and not regarded as earning her passage as the others were. She told herself fiercely she was being a fool, and that the fact she had been chosen by *Vision* as the representative was sufficient justification for her being there, but in her heart she knew she needed the reassurance of Shaun's approval, even if that was all she could ever have from him. She gave a little sigh and determinedly switched her attention back to Pablo and Francisco, who were crouched over the small pile of stones, concentrating on them as if their lives depended on it.

She was quietly pleased with the results of the session as she stored the film she had used and re-loaded her cameras later that morning. It was unlikely that she would do any more work at the camp itself, she thought. Her supplies of film, both for her movie camera and the two stills cameras she had brought, were of necessity limited and she wanted to save as much as possible for the journey to Ixtlacan and the ruins themselves. She re-packed her camera case, checking the various lenses she had brought with painstaking accuracy.

The pictures for *Vision* were in colour, and the film she had used already she packed in a special cooling box, ready for when the supply helicopter flew in later in the week. She had decided to try and develop some of her black and white material at the camp, but the equipment lacked the sophistication necessary for colour processing, and she had arranged to use a colour laboratory in Merida.

The only working problem that faced her now was obtaining the copy to go with her pictures, she thought ruefully. Since Shaun had so abruptly informed her that he would be taking Professor Morgan's place on the expedition that day at Chichen Itza, nothing had been said about this aspect of the assignment. She sighed. It could have been so easy, if she had only been able to approach him on equal terms as just another colleague. But that seemed impossible now. There was too much between them, and not just all the things that had been said and done. These, perhaps, were less telling than the silences, the deliberate reservations. All the time, James stood between them like a ghost. The thought brought her up sharply, her fingers suddenly clumsy on the straps of her bag. How was it she thought of James—like that—as if he no longer existed, when the truth was that the flesh and blood man might appear at any moment? She supposed that it was merely because of his long absence that James seemed to be coming less and less real in her mind. We'll be strangers when we meet again, she thought, and bit her lip as the realisation came home to her that they had never really been anything else.

She got up wearily, smoothing her damp hands down her thighs. She had never felt the ambivalence of her position so keenly as at that moment. The new depths she had sensed in herself under the compulsion of Shaun's lovemaking had exhilarated and alarmed her. As a married woman, she knew she had no right to feel such emotions and sensations in the arms of another man. She despised herself for being so weak, for allowing herself to be overcome by what could only be physical attraction. But was she being unfair to herself? she wondered despairingly. If she had been a real wife to James, with a normal happy marriage, wouldn't this have protected her—formed her shield and defence against other attractions, no matter how overwhelming? As it was, her first experience of adult passion had been with Shaun. It would be only too easy, too, to write him off as simply a predatory male who protected his own bachelor status by making a play for married women. He'd said himself that he persisted in forgetting that she was married, and she could believe him. She flushed slightly. She probably misled him by her own naïveté.

But was she deliberately deceiving herself, telling herself what she wanted to believe and shutting her eyes to the truth? Shaun most certainly did not share her inexperience with the opposite sex. Perhaps all he wanted was a light-hearted sophisticated affair, with her husband conveniently out of the way. Simply because his touch had aroused clamourings in her senses that she could neither assuage nor forget, this did not indicate that he necessarily felt the same. He was a man, after all, with needs that were franker and more physical than her own. He would not need any other emotional impetus than desire to embark upon the pursuit of a woman.

She needed to remember this and remain on her guard, she thought. No matter what she might feel, there was no future for her in any relationship with Shaun Lennox—just the basic fulfilment of a mutual need. And for her, that was no longer enough. She could acknowledge it now. For her there could be no easy giving to cure the pain that throbbed inside her. She wanted more than that, and the extent of her wanting frightened her.

If she was more than usually silent at lunch, little attention was paid to it by the others, who could talk of nothing but the next stage of the trip.

It was startling to realise that by this time the following day they would already be on their way. Gabrielle felt a slight shiver run through her. It was all so much a leap into the unknown. How would she cope now that she had all these emotional uncertainties to add to the everyday problems and dangers she would encounter? It wasn't too late, even yet. One hint that she didn't feel up to the journey would be enough. But even as the thought flitted across her mind, she knew nothing would prevail on her to draw back.

Besides, she told herself wryly, life never let you escape as easily as that. The day would inevitably come when she could not run any further.

No one was really surprised during the afternoon when it began to rain with heavy, monotonous persistence. Most of the party took refuge in the exhibits hut, treating it as a temporary club-house. Someone had a pack of cards, and the men played poker. Anna and Gabrielle were invited to join the game, but both of them declined. Anna read a book, but Gabrielle felt too restless to concentrate on anything, her nerves stretched almost to screaming point by the drumming of the rain on the corrugated roof.

She jumped violently as the door swung open and Shaun and Craig, who had been supervising the packing of the boats, to be used for the first stage of the trip, came in. Shaun was frowning darkly as he pulled his soaking poncho over his head.

'*Qu'avez vous, mon ami?* What is the matter?' Pierre Rosteau laid down his cards with a concerned expression.

Craig dropped into a vacant canvas chair at the table with a resigned expression. 'Felipe's turned up again,' he said grimly.

The silence that followed was almost tangibly awkward. Gabrielle glancing round questioningly, caught Anna's eye and was amazed to see the older woman look quickly away as if avoiding her gaze. And she wasn't the only one. Gabrielle realised that other furtive glances were being aimed at her, then hurriedly averted.

'*Ciel!*' Pierre turned to Shaun. 'But you will not permit him to stay. After what has happened . . .'

'He's staying.' Shaun walked across to where a pot of coffee was keeping warm on a spirit stove. He poured some of the dark, bitter brew into a tin mug and drank, his eyes fixed steadily on Pierre over the rim of the mug.

There was a chorus of protest, but he dominated it easily, his voice calm and cold.

'I suspected he'd—make contact sooner or later. The sooner the better as far as I'm concerned. If he comes with us, we can at least keep an eye on him. Besides, he's a spare hand with a paddle and from what Pablo tells me we're going to need all the help we can get. It's been reasonably dry here, I know, but it's been raining almost continuously up-river and the Rio is swollen. We can't anticipate a very pleasant trip.'

As he spoke, his eyes met Gabrielle's. Her chin went up immediately. Nothing would make her show him that she was afraid, although some of the others were openly grimacing apprehensively at the prospect confronting them.

'Well, maybe.' Craig sounded mutinous. 'But I wouldn't let that sonofabitch within miles of the expedition. We know what he is . . .'

'Exactly.' Shaun drained the dregs of the coffee and replaced the mug on the table. 'We know—and he knows it too. So why is he here?'

Pierre shrugged expansively. '*Peut-être, mon ami*, he hopes that we shall forgive—and forget.'

'Hardly likely.' Shaun pulled a chair towards him with his foot and dropped on to its seat, his arms folded loosely across its back. 'No, he wants something, if I'm any judge, and I could stand knowing precisely what it is. If we kick him out, we'll never know.'

There was a long pause, then Anna stood up. 'You're the boss,' she said decisively. 'And at least this time we've been warned.'

There was a reluctant murmur of assent from the others, and once again Gabrielle felt absurdly self-conscious. Her bewilderment grew. Who was this Felipe, and what had he done to rouse all this antagonism? And how was she involved in all this? She knew she hadn't imagined the embarrassed sidelong glances that had been coming her way while Shaun and the others were arguing. She got up quickly, the leg of her chair scraping across the floor.

'I think the rain's stopped,' she said too loudly. 'I think I'll get some air.'

I'm sure you have a lot to talk about, she added silently.

Outside, it was like stepping into a steam bath, and the smell of dank, rotting vegetation caught in her throat. She paused for a moment, looking with distaste at the sodden ground she had to cross to reach her own hut. Above her head, brassy, menacing clouds hung, hinting that the rain had not done with them yet. She felt the warm damp penetrating her clothing as she stood there, and she gritted her teeth as she stepped gingerly down on to the saturated earth.

Her hand was on the door of her hut when a voice said, 'Señora Warner?'

She turned, amazed. A small man was standing, smiling ingratiatingly at her. At first glance, she thought he was one of the *chicleros*, but then she noticed that instead of the loose cotton shirt and pants that they wore, he had on a light-weight tropical suit which fitted him rather too well, and a soft, expensive-looking Panama hat.

'Who are you?' she asked in Spanish.

'Me llamo Felipe, señora.'

So this was the new and unpopular arrival. Gabrielle found him unprepossessing, with his thin black moustache and too-ready smile.

'How do you do?' she said awkwardly, and turned away again, intending to go into the hut.

'Wait, *señora.* I have message.' His English was poor, but it was comprehensible, and she felt her stomach lurch crazily.

'A message? For me?'

'Si, señora.' He was almost preening himself. 'I have to tell you, you must come at once. *Es urgente.* He wait for you.'

'Who's waiting for me?' Gabrielle looked around,

dazedly. 'What are you talking about? Where must I go? who wants me?'

The sallow face looked almost reproachful. 'Don Jaime, *señora.* Who else should it be? He says you must go to him. *Es importante.*'

'Don Jaime!' Gabrielle's lips barely parted as she whispered the words. She gazed in disbelief at the small figure confronting her. Had her summons from James finally come from this unlikely source—a man no one else seemed to trust? She gathered her scattered wits. 'What else did he say?'

But Felipe had no further confidences for her, it seemed. His eyes flicked sideways with swift furtiveness, like a hunted animal startled by a sudden noise, then he slid round the side of the hut and disappeared.

She was dazed by the suddenness of it all, her mouth dry, her heart pounding. Yet she still hadn't the slightest idea where James was. Presumably she would have to trust this Felipe sufficiently for him to take her to James. She felt nauseated at the prospect. And why had he vanished like that when he must have known she had a dozen questions to ask him?

A slight sound behind her made her whirl round apprehensively and she had her answer. Shaun was standing on the small verandah which ran round the exhibits hut. He was lighting a cheroot, his entire concentration seemingly centred on this mundane task, but as she watched, he raised his head and their glances met and locked. If she had ever doubted that he had seen her talking to Felipe, those doubts were dispelled for ever. His gaze was searingly contemptuous, asking for no explanation nor apparently desiring one, merely condemning her out of hand. She stared back at him mutely, her mouth trembling, as he flicked the spent match away from him into some nearby undergrowth. Then he turned and went back into the exhibits hut.

Gabrielle turned and felt blindly for the latch of her door. She made her way across the small room to the stark sanctuary of her bed, and sank down on it, shaking uncontrollably.

For good or ill, it seemed that James had come back into her life. A slow, burning tear trickled down the curve of her cheek and she wiped it away fiercely with the back of her hand, damming back the tide of emotion that was threatening to overwhelm her.

She lay down on the bed, burying her face in the hard pillow, while her head throbbed and bright lights burned and danced behind her closed eyelids.

She lay for a long time, trying to come to terms with this new development, attempting to persuade herself that it was all for the best.

And deep inside her, a small voice she could not control whispered, 'Goodbye, my love. Goodbye, my love,' over and over again, until she thought her heart would burst with the pain of it.

CHAPTER SIX

GABRIELLE sat in the bow of the boat, her shoulders hunched under the thin waterproof cape which had become a permanent part of her attire since they had embarked the previous day. Not that anything was proof against the rain, which seemed to penetrate even the most secure covering, she thought tiredly. And when the rain stopped, as it had now, there was this dank, warm mist rising from the brown river and seeping through to your very skin. It was like breathing through a blanket.

Yesterday, when they had still been on the Usamacinta, it had all somehow seemed more cheerful, in spite of the weather. Pablo and Francisco had sung as they paddled, and there had been jokes and shouted remarks from one boat to the other. Camping at night had seemed fun too, with Pablo showing them how to cut leaves with their machetes, and build the *champas* which would provide their hammocks with shelter during the night. Gabrielle had not cared too much for the tinned stew which had been served up for supper round the fire, but Anna assured her that as soon as they left the river and started to trek through the jungle, their diet would be supplemented by fresh meat and game.

But as soon as they had left the Usamacinta, the whole atmosphere had changed. There was no singing, no laughter, only the rhythmic splash and dip of the paddles, and an occasional barked word of warning as someone spotted a submerged tree. No one needed to tell Gabrielle that this was the Rio Torcido—the Accursed River. She had seen Pablo lay down his paddle and cross himself fervently at the start of the journey. And now there was this odd hush, as if the evil that ruled here could be placated by silence. It was a disturbing thought, and she shivered involuntarily. She was quietly thankful that she was not in the leading boat, although she despised herself for her cowardice. Anna seemed to have no such qualms, she thought enviously. But she was under no illusions that Shaun Lennox had designated her to travel in the second boat for any chivalrous reason. A bitter little smile curved her mouth. Since they had set out on this journey she had not had a single opportunity to speak with Felipe alone. Yesterday they had been in separate boats as well, and at the camp, Gabrielle had realised with mounting indignation that there was invariably someone at her elbow. It was all very casual and friendly—the apparent concern of old hands for a newcomer to the rain forest—but it did not alter the fact that she was being watched. For a time she had toyed with the notion of going to Shaun Lennox and demanding an explanation, but the memory of the contempt in his eyes provided an active deterrent.

If it had been anyone else, she thought, it would have been a simple matter to explain that Felipe had brought her a message from James. But the thought of having to present Shaun with such information was more painful than she could bear. Paradoxically, it was his indifference she feared more than anything else. Supposing he simply did not care that James had come back into her life? How would she be able to bear it? She tried to brace herself by mentally reminding herself that she was at a low ebb in her morale, as well as being physically jaded by the all-pervading humidity. But at the same time she knew unhappily that all tiredness and discomfort would be forgotten if Shaun's arms were to open to her once more.

She bit her lip savagely. She must not think like that, she reproached herself. James existed—her husband legally, if nothing more, and entitled to her loyalty, even if he had not behaved with equal consideration towards her.

The fact that Felipe was the last person in the world she would have chosen as an ally only served to increase her bitterness. What had possessed James to use him as a messenger? she wondered. And why did her contact with James have to be conducted under such apparent secrecy? She hunched her shoulders irritably. Well, she would go along with it only as far as she had to, but she wouldn't make any approaches to Felipe. She was tired of secrets and silences and hostile atmospheres she did not understand.

And what was so urgent or important that it demanded her presence at James' side after these weeks of silence? she asked herself, her mouth twisting drily. The only matter of importance they had to discuss as far as she was concerned was this travesty of a marriage, and their respective futures, but there was little urgency about it, she thought, pain and bitterness twisting inside her again.

A warning shout from the leading boat jolted her from her reverie, and she heard Craig who was sitting behind her curse softly under his breath, and order the men to stop paddling. Both boats swung in towards the bank, and when they were moored securely, the occupants began to clamber out, stretching stiffened limbs. Gabrielle, slipping in a patch of mud, caught at a nearby tree to steady herself and gasped in pain as hidden thorns tore at the palm of her hand. She looked at the dark spots of blood welling up with consternation. The dangers of blood poisoning had been reiterated by the others time and time again during the preparations for the expedition, but she was reluctant to make a fuss about such a relatively minor incident. She had a few antiseptic dressings in her pack, and some tweezers to remove the remnants of thorn. She would have to make do with that.

'Welcome to dry land.' Anna wandered up to her.

'Is that what it is?' Gabrielle cast a comprehensive glance around her, and Anna laughed.

'Maybe calling it dry is a bit of an exaggeration, but at least it doesn't move!'

'Why have we stopped?' Gabrielle looked towards the water's edge where Pierre, Craig, and some of the others were in earnest conference with Shaun.

'Can't you hear?' Anna looked at her with faint amusement. 'It's a good job we didn't have you as look-out!'

Gabrielle bent her head, listening intently. Somewhere in the distance she was aware of a faint roaring noise, but she was unable to guess at its origin. She looked enquiringly at Anna.

'A waterfall,' Anna explained. 'Probably quite a big one.'

'What happens now?' Gabrielle could not help a stir of excitement. 'Do we shoot the rapids?'

Anna cast her eyes to heaven. 'Thanks—but no, thanks. I don't think you'll want to once you see it either. No, I'm afraid it's donkey work. We'll have to carry the boats and stores along the bank until we get past. We're lucky really that it hasn't happened before.'

'It's not really my idea of luck,' Gabrielle said drily.

The thought of having to carry extra loads with her sore hand was not an appealing one either. She waited until Anna moved away, then rummaged inside her waterproof for a clean handkerchief, which she twisted round her hand, using her teeth to fasten the knot. It was rough and ready, but it would have to do until she had the time and the privacy for more adequate treatment.

She thrust her hand hastily behind her back as Shaun Lennox came striding towards her. It occurred to her with a pang that this was the first time he had approached her since he had witnessed her conversation with Felipe, but it was soon obvious that he had not come to make any friendly overtures. His face seemed carved from granite, and his eyes were like pale steel.

'This is where you stop being a passenger, Mrs Warner,' he began without preamble. 'You're not expected to help carry the boat, but you'll have to be responsible for your own equipment, and give a hand with the other stuff as well.'

She had flushed with indignation at the implication in his words that she would not be prepared to pull her weight on the trip, but before she could retort, he had turned on his heel and walked away.

Gabrielle fumed inwardly as she made her way awkwardly down to the boat. Her camera case, wrapped in a polythene sheet, she had stored under the thin plank which served as a seat. She unwrapped it now, noticing with concern that in spite of her care the clasps and hinges were already rusting, and pulled the strap over her shoulder, before seeking out Pierre and offering her services as a porter. He fussed over her almost paternally, insisting that she take one of the smaller packs, and adjusting it so that it balanced comfortably across her shoulders. To her embarrassment, Shaun was standing not far away and she wished Pierre was not so keen to make concessions to her sex and slender build. She wanted to make him swallow his sneer about her being a 'passenger' on the trip.

The journey along the bank was a nightmare. The slippery ground was a trap for the unwary, and fallen branches and huge twisted roots turned their passage into an obstacle race. At one point, the bank had slipped away completely into the river, and they had to make their way slowly across the gap using the protruding roots of a giant tree which reached out across the now turbulent waters.

The noise from the cascade was getting louder, but Gabrielle was too preoccupied with maintaining her footing to look around her. Her shoulders ached from their unaccustomed burden and she was thankful when someone called a halt.

The river was a magnificent sight. No longer brown and placid, it boiled and swirled in a mass of foam down a twisted network of steps and passages forged in the rock.

It was savage and compelling, and Gabrielle wriggled free of her pack, reaching eagerly for her camera case. She was engrossed in her task when Shaun's voice interrupted her.

'We haven't time for aesthetics, Mrs Warner. We have work to do and not many more hours of daylight to do it in.'

'I also have work to do, Dr Lennox.' She tried to make her voice as icily formal as his own. 'May I remind you that I'm not simply here to take pictures for my magazine but to provide a photographic record of this journey for the Institute. This wasn't my condition, but Professor Morgan's.'

He looked her over in silence, his lips compressed. 'Am I supposed to be impressed by all this devotion to duty?' he asked eventually.

'Impressing you isn't part of the agreement, either.' The words were defiant enough, but her spirit ached. 'But I'm sorry if I'm—holding up the convoy. I've finished now.'

She bent her head, concentrating fiercely on stowing her camera back in its case, sensing not seeing that he had walked away. It would have been more convenient to have walked with the camera slung round her neck for ease of access, but the most urgent necessity was to keep it as dry as possible. She wondered rather wearily how her film would stand up to the heat and damp, and promised herself a developing session with the rolls of black and white film she had already used as soon as she got back to the base camp.

It was a relief to leave the roaring water behind them, but they had to walk nearly a mile over the slippery, treacherous ground before it was safe to put the boats back in the river. Gabrielle's own dejection passed unnoticed in the general air of weariness and apathy which had beset the party. The cascades had been an unexpected setback and had cost several precious hours to negotiate, and everyone was tight-lipped, grim, and mud-stained as they climbed back into the boats. Gabrielle was aware of a swift sullen look from Felipe as he scrambled back into his place, his once smart suit soiled and crumpled.

Her hand was throbbing, and she unwrapped her handkerchief unobtrusively and looked at it. The punctures left by the thorns were red and angry, and she was irritated by her own carelessness. Craig, she knew, would wait while she attended to her hand, but Shaun would want to know the reason for the delay, and she could not face the thought of another confrontation with him, and having to endure his scorn.

Even if her hand festered and fell off, she wouldn't let him accuse her of needlessly holding up the expedition again, she thought rebelliously.

It seemed like a good resolution at the time, but by the time they had reached the spot where they were to camp for the night, and the *champas* had been built, and the cooking fires coaxed into life, she had begun to wish she had swallowed her pride. She found a secluded place away from the fire, and opened the tin of dressings she had recovered from her pack. They now looked woefully inadequate for her swollen hand, and it wasn't easy to cope with the protective coverings single-handed. She winced as she pressed the dressing into place. She was sure there were pieces of thorn left in the wounds, but there wasn't sufficient light for her to either see them or deal with them. That would have to wait until one of their rest stops on the following day, she thought despondently.

She slept badly and woke feeling heavy and lethargic, but she was relieved to see that her hand had not swollen any more, and she was able to help Anna prepare the morning meal without drawing attention to it. Today they were turning inland, leaving the boats pulled up on the bank, and Gabrielle decided that it was of life's little ironies that she now found the tedium of the boat journey of the previous two days infinitely preferable to the walk that now faced her.

A few hours later she was no longer capable even of appreciating the irony of the situation. When Shaun finally called a halt, she sank down on a fallen tree trunk, reaching like an automaton for her water canteen. The liquid it contained was tepid and tasted strongly of the tablets used to purify it, but it moistened her burning mouth and throat, and she tipped some into her uninjured hand, pouring it over her temples, and down her neck into the opening of her shirt. The wide straw hat she was wearing seemed to have tightened round her head like an iron band, but her legs no longer seemed to belong to her.

'What you lose on the roundabouts,' she murmured, and heard herself giggle, a stupidly inane sound which seemed to echo in her ears.

'Gabrielle.' Firm hands removed the iron band, and her head felt light—so light that it might float away above the tangle of trees and vines and find the sun that surely still existed somewhere above this malevolent green wilderness.

'Gabrielle!' The familiar voice was imperative now, and something stung her cheeks sharply. She cried out and looked up dazedly into Shaun's blazing eyes.

'What's the matter with you?' he demanded. He was angry again, she could see that, but there was something else in his face too. He looked worried.

Oh, he'd be worried all right—worried in case his precious expedition was held up again. She got to her feet with dignity and would have fallen without his supporting arm.

'I'm quite all right, Dr Lennox,' she spoke with care. 'I'm quite ready to go on.'

'Show me your hand.' His voice was murderously soft and it never occurred to her to disobey. Mutely she extended her palm and heard him swear quietly and obscenely under his breath. He lowered her back to the tree trunk, and she closed her eyes as the trees and his tall figure danced in front of them in some weird miasma.

She was never quite sure what happened after that. There was pain, she knew, so sharp and piercing that the world slid away. When it returned, it was dark and she was lying in her hammock with a camp fire flickering somewhere nearby. Someone brought her a mug of coffee and she drank it thirstily, and fell asleep again almost at once.

'You gave us quite a fright,' said Anna.

Gabrielle opened her eyes and stared up at her drowsily. 'What happened?' she asked.

'You poisoned your hand.' Anna made it sound an everyday occurrence. 'Shaun had to lance it. He'll be along in a minute to put on a fresh dressing.' She smiled faintly. 'I came on ahead in case you wanted to put some clothes on and needed help.'

For the first time, Gabrielle realised she was naked inside her sleeping bag. Anna gave her shoulder a reassuring pat.

'Don't look so stricken. You were running a slight fever. Shaun and I took turns to sponge you down. We hung your clothes beside the fire all night, so you should be the driest person on the expedition!'

Talking gently, she eased Gabrielle into her shirt and handed her the crumpled jeans. Gabrielle was amazed at how well she felt now the initial drowsiness had worn off, and she suspected there had been more than coffee in that bedtime drink the night before. Her hand felt sore, but that dreadful throbbing had stopped and she could move her fingers without discomfort.

She was experimentally clenching and unclenching her fist when Shaun arrived.

'You'll live,' he said succinctly as he fastened her bandage, and she flushed slightly.

'I'm very grateful to you,' she said haltingly.

'In that case, if you need medical attention again on

this trip, perhaps you'll ask for it and not try to be a heroine. You're not cutting your finger in your hygienic London kitchen now, with a Health Service casualty department just down the road.' His tone was grim, but it contained none of the anger and contempt of the past few days.

'I didn't want to be a nuisance,' she mumbled, and heard him give a swift, impatient sigh.

'Better that than a potential stretcher case.' He glanced at his watch. 'Do you feel well enough to travel? If so, I'd like to make a start in an hour. According to Pablo we should reach Ixtlacan this afternoon.'

'I'm well enough to travel,' she said instantly, and drew a wry smile from him.

'Remember what I said about heroism,' he told her, and stood up. He paused for a moment and looked down at her, the expression on his face unreadable. 'Gabrielle, I want you to know this. Neither you nor James have anything to fear from me now or in the future. I hope that sets your mind at rest.' He turned and walked away before she could formulate any kind of response. A sudden weakness possessed her body and she lay back again, fighting tears. This sudden, unexpected kindness and consideration was even harder to bear than his hostility. It was too vivid a reminder of what their relationship might have been, and she mustn't think about that.

No, I've nothing to fear, she cried inwardly. Nothing but being alone.

She was calm by the time the hammocks had been dismantled and stowed away in the packs. She was not the only casualty, she discovered. Pierre had developed a painful blister on his left heel, and Martin Forster, one of the other Americans, had fallen foul of an ants' nest and was nursing a crop of nasty-looking red blotches. But in spite of these minor nuisances, the depression of the day before seemed to have lifted from everyone. They were within striking distance of their goal and they knew it, and while an element of tension remained, the atmosphere was basically optimistic.

The going was rough and progress, of necessity, was slow. What track there was had become overgrown since Pablo and Francisco had last passed that way, and the party had stopped at frequent intervals while a way was hacked through with machetes. Gabrielle noticed that both Shaun and Craig were carrying guns that had been unslung from the packs, and assumed they were on the look-out for the game to supplement the rather tedious diet of tinned stew, corned beef and pemmican, but Pierre with whom she was walking soon disillusioned her.

'Estoleros, ma petite,' he said briefly, and Gabrielle felt a chill run down her spine, as she remembered the things Shaun had told her about the site robbers.

'Do you think they know about Ixtlacan?' she asked diffidently, and was surprised to see Pierre's normally cheerful face look grim as he turned to her.

'Don't you know?' he asked coldly, then broke off abruptly as though aware he had said too much.

Gabrielle's eyes widened. 'What do you mean? Pierre, you must tell me. There's something wrong, isn't there, and you think I know about it.'

He hesitated fractionally, then shrugged. 'Forget it, *chérie*. Who knows what we will find at Ixtlacan, or whom.'

'You're dodging the issue,' she accused, dragging at his arm, but his mouth was clamped tightly shut and it was evident he had no intention of saying any more. There was an awkward pause, and then he began to chat again with some of his usual ebullience, pointing out a clump of vivid pink flowers, like lilies, and telling her the names of some of the trees they were passing.

Gabrielle only paid his remarks the modicum of attention. Her thoughts were churning madly, and a terrible suspicion was growing in her mind. Somehow, and soon, she had to get hold of Felipe. She might get the truth from him, which no one else seemed willing to tell her.

The opportunity came sooner than she had expected, when Shaun called a rest stop. She drank thirstily from her canteen, looking warily round her, but the others seemed to be enjoying their brief relaxation and she was not under surveillance.

She put the stopper back in her canteen and unfastened her camera case, taking out her own Pentax. Then, trying to behave casually, she wandered away from the main party. A few yards back she had noticed a large bush almost covered in vivid scarlet berries which she would photograph. As she adjusted her camera, she saw that Felipe, who was sitting on his own, had risen silently and slipped into the neighbouring thicket as if he was going to obey a call of nature.

She waited in almost painful suspense, staring at the bush, and expecting at any moment for her absence to be noticed. At last, just as she had decided she would have to take her picture and return to the group, she heard his voice. '*Señora!*'

This is crazy, she thought.

'What do you want?' she said steadily.

'You must go to Don Jaime, *señora*.' There was almost painful urgency in Felipe's whispering voice. 'You must go quickly—tell no one. *Es muy urgente*.'

She lifted the Pentax and photographed the bush as if she was a novice who had never held a camera before. 'How can I go to Don Jaime? I can't be alone in the forest.'

'Felipe will go with the *señora*.'

'*Muy bien*,' she said. Her throat felt stiff. 'When do we go?'

'Tonight, *señora*,' said the hidden whisper. 'We go to-night.'

'Tonight,' she agreed, and turned away.

'Beware of the berries, *chérie*.' Pierre was approaching.

'It is a pretty bush, *non*, but its beauty hides danger and death.'

Gabrielle looked at him sharply, wondering if his words could be construed in two different ways, but his smile was bland and innocent and she relaxed imperceptibly.

'Don't worry about me, Pierre,' she said lightly. 'I don't intend to take any more risks.'

It was about an hour later that Shaun called another halt. She sank down on a patch of rough undergrowth, keeping a wary eye open for ants and other horrors, and closed her eyes, fanning herself with her hat. She was surprised to hear her name being called. When she looked up, Craig was beckoning to her. She got slowly to her feet, brushing dead leaves and grasses from her jeans, and went to meet him. His face was wreathed in smiles.

'Got your camera handy, honey?' he asked.

Then she realised.

'We're—actually there?'

'We actually are.' He pushed her gently up the track. 'Hey, Shaun, convince the lady!'

She seemed to be travelling up a narrow tunnel of trees. It was dark and very quiet. And then the undergrowth suddenly stopped and she scrambled across the dried bed of a stream into the clearing.

At first sight it was like a small tree-covered hill, about fifty feet high, then, as she approached, she realised with a sense of growing excitement that the mound was not composed of earth but of cut stones.

'Yes, it's a pyramid,' Shaun said beside her. 'The temple on top has crumbled, but there are other pyramids, and one of them looks from its shape as though its temple is still there.'

She knew as she began to climb that he was coming with her. The loose stones shifted under her feet and bounced back down the slope, but she had no sensation of fear. She was panting when she reached the top, but all weariness fell away in sheer exhilaration as she stared down at the forest and around her at the remains of the city. There were eight pyramids in all, she counted, set broadly in a shallow rectangle, and it was the tallest one—nearly eighty or ninety feet high, she estimated—that still carried the temple.

Slowly and almost ceremoniously she lifted both her arms towards the sky.

'What are you doing?' Shaun had sat down on a pile of loose rocks and lit a cheroot.

'Paying homage to the sun,' she said gaily, half-hysterical with wonder and excitement.

'Take care. If Anna's right, this city was dedicated to Ixchel, his wife. She might get jealous.'

'Not if she loved him. She did, didn't she?'

He blew a smoke ring. 'That's a debatable point. Some of the stories about her say she was a wanton, cruel, lustful and incapable of being faithful to her husband. Not a very attractive character.'

'No,' Gabrielle said woodenly.

He got up, stretching. She could feel he was looking at her. All her senses seemed heightened suddenly, and she had never been so conscious of another human being in her life.

'If ever you feel like paying homage to the goddess,' he said slowly, 'you could always tell me.'

She was very still, her pulses fluttering like stricken birds.

'Why?' she asked at last. 'Is it because you think I'm like her—wanton and incapable of—fidelity?' She almost choked on the word.

'What I forgot to mention,' he said quietly, 'was that she was also very beautiful.'

He threw away the partly smoked cheroot with a kind of

controlled violence and started back down the slope, his boots slithering on the stones.

The camp was already being constructed at the edge of the clearing when Gabrielle descended, and she had, perforce, to be caught up in the general burst of activity which had suddenly possessed the entire party, weariness, scratches and blisters forgotten. Even if she could not entirely share the general jubilation, she could sympathise with it, particularly as it seemed that this time they had reached a site before the *esteleros*. Anna had already taken a preliminary inspection of some of the giant obelisks in front of the pyramids, and found that they were intact, and Craig had already been in radio contact with the base camp, arranging for the supply helicopter to fly in the equipment they needed to lift the stelae, many of which had fallen over into the undergrowth, and to make latex moulds of them.

Pablo and Francisco were already hard at work clearing away the encroaching trees and undergrowth to provide a landing space for the helicopter.

Work could be her salvation too, Gabrielle decided. She took pictures of the pyramids, and climbed again to the top of one to photograph the jungle from its roof. Then, using the special lens for close work, she began to photograph some of the carvings on the stelae under Anna's direction. It occurred to her as she worked that this might be her sole contribution to the expedition and she took almost exaggerated care to ensure it was as near perfect as she could make it.

What did James want of her? she wondered, as she exchanged a used roll of film for a fresh one. And, what was more important, would he allow her to return to the expedition to complete her assignment? She bit her lip. If the suspicions she was harbouring were correct, it was unlikely, so she would not simply be letting Professor Morgan down but the magazine as well. This would inevitably mean that she would find herself out of a job when she got back to the United Kingdom. It was a bleak prospect, and a long, bitter sigh escaped her. What a mess everything had become, she thought wearily, and there was no clear solution to any of it. She could come to no decision at all until she had seen James, however reluctant she might feel about their coming meeting.

'Gabrielle.' Anna came scrambling to her side, her rather pale face glowing. 'Shaun is going to try and open the temple before it gets dark. Come on!'

They climbed slowly and steadily, respecting the danger of the steep and crumbling steps which led with a kind of majestic inevitability to the squat building at their summit. Pierre and Martin were already at work with machetes, clearing the strangling vines from the narrow entrance and its elaborately carved columns. The damp and encroaching foliage had not completely obliterated the savagery of the scenes they depicted—Pipil the sun god, and Ixchel, goddess of the moon, receiving sacrifice—their victims' bodies bent like bowstrings over the altar while their still-beating hearts were torn out of them. Gabrielle swallowed, fighting down an instinctive feeling of revulsion. Pierre, noticing her sudden pallor, gave her waist a comforting squeeze.

'*Autre temps, autre moeurs, ma chère,*' he whispered. 'Never forget, the victims thought it an honour to be chosen for the gods. They went to their deaths accompanied by singers and flute players, wearing their finest clothes and jewels.'

She nodded and managed a faint smile, then ducking her head, followed the others into the darkness beyond the low entrance. For a moment she stood still, as her eyes adjusted to the darkness, then Shaun and Craig switched on their powerful electric torches and began a systematic sweep of the roof and walls. There was a smell of damp and mould, and a large fruit bat disturbed by the sudden light began to swoop in and out of the shadows, making Gabrielle glad that her hair was scooped up inside her wide-brimmed hat. The temple chamber appeared to be empty, but as the torches reached floor level, they heard a sudden cry of excitement from Craig, and Shaun's voice unemotionally bidding him to hold the torch steady.

A great stone slab had been displaced, revealing a dark hollow beneath it. Beside it, as if standing guard, was a huge stone jaguar, its paw raised in menace.

'Take care! We don't know how safe this floor is,' Shaun warned sharply, as Craig dropped on to his knees and began to crawl towards the edge.

'It's O.K.' Craig's voice was breathless as he peered down into the darkness. 'Let's have those torches over here. I think I can see something.'

The silence was almost tangible as they waited for his next words. But when they came, his voice was flat with disappointment.

'This is it, all right. There's a complete skeleton down here, but that's all. Someone's been here before us—the death mask, the ornaments have gone.'

A groan of disappointment went up, and Shaun cursed savagely under his breath.

'I don't understand.' Gabrielle turned to Pierre. 'What were they expecting to find?'

'What they have found, *chérie*—a grave.' Pierre sounded thoroughly despondent. 'There has been a theory that many of the pyramids were built to house tombs for Mayan princes and high priests. Such men would be buried with masks of jade, with pottery and jewels.'

Gabrielle's heart was beating painfully. 'And someone else has been here—has stolen these things?'

'It seems so.' Pierre sighed. 'The grave was open, and only the poor bones remain. A rich haul—for somebody.'

She turned away, sick at heart, wanting to get outside again into the sunshine, out of this place of death. The others were all clustered round the open grave, staring down into it. Her absence would not be missed.

Supper that night was a far cry from the jubilant affair that had been planned. Pablo had shot some pheasants, and they roasted them on spits over the fire, but even this unusual addition to the menu could make much headway against the prevailing air of gloom. It was obvious, Gabrielle realised, that they felt they had been shown a glimpse of one of the really glittering prizes of archaeology, only to have it snatched away at the last minute. Even the stelae, and the carvings on the temple itself, now seemed inevitably second best. To add to the general bitterness, Craig had actually picked up two fragments of jade from the skeleton, which the thieves had apparently overlooked, proving that the treasures had really existed, and were not merely wishful thinking.

'It's sickening to think that we'll never know how late we were,' Anna said to Gabrielle in an undertone, as they drank their coffee. 'It could be weeks, of course, but it might just be a matter of hours. Oh, I can't bear to think about it!'

Gabrielle forced herself to murmur something in reply. She felt emotionally drained, and the thought of the journey ahead of her and the encounter with James at the end of it made her nervous almost to the point of sickness. She wanted desperately to shift the burden of the knowledge that had been unwillingly forced on her to someone else.

She sat alone, after Anna had drifted away to talk to Martin and Craig, staring into the flickering flames and trying to decide what she would say to James when she finally came up with him. She was all ready to slip away when Felipe gave the word. She had stored her exposed film in watertight cartons and labelled it for the processing laboratory. She had given it to Craig to put on the supply helicopter when it arrived, and he had accepted her rather lame excuse that she might be in the middle of a photographic session when the helicopter arrived. She had filled her canteen with drinking water, and taken a few tins of food from the stores. She wondered drearily how long it would take to get to James, wherever he had gone to ground. Surely Felipe would have warned her if it had been a long journey.

Her heart leapt agonisingly as firm footsteps sounded on the loose stones and Shaun Lennox came up to her. He was carrying a first aid kit.

'Your hand needs a fresh dressing,' he said abruptly, squatting down at her side. Gabrielle braced herself to endure the cool impersonality of his touch, and flushed slightly as she met his level gaze.

'Did I hurt you?' he asked coldly, and she knew he had been fully aware that she had flinched away from him. She supposed she should be thankful that he did not guess the truth, that she would soon be gone, taking with her the shame of the need that the slightest brush of his fingers had the power to arouse in her. Her body ached for the fulfilment his kisses had promised.

He changed the dressing, and applied a new bandage, his fingers meticulously efficient, as if she was a stranger they had never touched in desire.

She sat, tongue-tied with misery, waiting for him to depart, bitterly aware that she would not be able even to say goodbye to him, except in her heart. But he didn't leave her at once, as she had expected. He remained for a while, squatting back on his heels, his dark brows drawn together in a brooding look. Finally he sighed, as if rousing himself, and thrust a hand into his pants pocket.

'I picked this up in the temple today,' he said abruptly. 'I haven't shown it to anyone else, and I don't intend to mention it either. You'll probably recognise it.'

It was a man's watch, the gold strap hanging broken and the glass smashed. Gabrielle knew it at once.

'Thank you,' she said tonelessly, as he put it into her hand.

'Oh, God!' The words seemed ground out of him. 'Of all the women in the world, Gabrielle, why does it have to be you?'

His mouth found hers with a savage completeness that wiped out every other emotion. She was aware of nothing but the longing to surrender to him, body and soul, but before she could even lift her arms to cling to him, he had let her go, getting to his feet in one lithe movement. She pressed her hand convulsively to her mouth as his dark figure disappeared swiftly in the shadows. His mouth burning hers would be yet another memory to take with her tonight, she thought desolately. But how could she live the rest of her life on memories?

CHAPTER SEVEN

SEATED on her pack, leaning against the low wall which some Mayan mason had built centuries before to mark the boundary of his city, Gabrielle stared up at the brilliant moon, and wondered if it was an omen. Was Ixchel walking the heavens to remind the intruders in her ruined city that she still ruled there? she asked herself half-mockingly. If so, this was one night when her presence could have been dispensed with. Gabrielle had felt exposed and vulnerable in the moonlight as she had crept out of her hammock, and collected her pack from the patch of undergrowth where she had hidden it earlier. She had moved silently as a shadow, tensing at every unguarded movement, in case someone else in the party was as wakeful as she was.

Of Felipe there had been no sign, apart from the grubby scrap of paper that had been pushed into her bedroll, telling her in a few ill-spelled words the time and place of their rendezvous. Gabrielle, unable to sleep, had been early for the appointment, and she was glad.

Ixtlacan in moonlight made an unforgettable sight, and it was a wrench to think she might never see it again or capture any more of its primitive dignity on film. She allowed herself deliberately to fret over her uncompleted work, and the problems the abandonment of her assignment would cause in an effort to hold a greater anguish at a distance. It could even be that the amount of film she had taken already could prove adequate for the *Vision* feature. But would Shaun still provide the promised written accompaniment, in view of her defection from the expedition? She squared her shoulders briefly. That was something over which she would have no more influence after tonight.

Her head came up sharply, registering a stealthy movement somewhere to her left. She held her breath for a moment, then relaxed as Felipe's small figure hunched into view. He was bowed under a large pack, and a machete was tucked into an improvised rope belt round his middle. He was very different from the dapper figure she had met at the base camp, she thought with a feeling of inexplicable satisfaction.

'*Señora*?' he hissed at her. 'You were not seen?'

'Of course not,' she whispered back. 'Were you?'

He muttered something under his breath and shot her a look of real malevolence. Gabrielle stared at him uneasily. She neither liked nor particularly trusted him, but so far she had not regarded him as an enemy. Now she was not so sure, and this journey took on a new and even more alarming dimension.

He waited with barely controlled impatience as she put on her pack, and picked up her camera case. His eyes snapped furiously as they took in this last item:

'Why you bring that?'

Gabrielle was taken aback. 'They're my cameras—and they're valuable,' she replied shortly, regretting the words almost as soon as they were uttered. It might have been better not to let someone like Felipe know she had anything of value with her, she thought wryly, but his reaction, although violent, was somewhat reassuring.

'You leave them here,' he whispered, with an angry gesture. 'We don't need them. No cameras. No pictures. We go quickly—carry little.'

'I'm certainly not leaving them,' Gabrielle retorted. 'One of them doesn't even belong to me, but to the magazine I work for. And no one is asking you to carry them. I can manage perfectly well.'

'They not go. They stay here.' Felipe seemed about to stamp with rage.

'Then I stay too,' she said coolly. 'I have work to do here—*muy urgente, muy importante*. Perhaps you'd like to tell Don Jaime that.'

For a moment she wondered detachedly if he was actually going to burst, but then, as if making an immense effort, he seemed to calm himself, sending her an ingratiating smile.

'No, we take—we go. Now we must hurry, *señora*.'

She waited for him to lead the way, then realised he seemed to be waiting for her to go first—a courtesy she hadn't expected from him. The darkness of the forest swallowed them up, blotting out the moonlight. Gabrielle was thankful when Felipe produced a small torch and sent its beam up the track they were taking. They were among the creatures of the night now, she thought fearfully, hunters and prey under the forest's cloak. Every rustle in the undergrowth lifted the hair on the back of her neck, and her only consolation was that Felipe seemed to have even less confidence in these alien surroundings than she did. He crossed himself repeatedly as they stumbled along, muttering invocations to a variety of saints, none of whom sounded familiar to Gabrielle. She sighed, thinking that Felipe's abilities as a guide were another addition to the list of shortcoming she could compile about him.

They had been walking for over an hour when she called a halt. Progress by day in this sort of terrain was of necessity slow and painful, but at night it was infinitely worse. But Felipe seemed oddly reluctant to take a breather, and she found she had to insist quite forcibly. She realised with growing alarm that Felipe's fear was that they might be followed, and in some way prevented from completing their journey. She did not attempt to argue with him or reassure him, knowing that her Spanish would not be equal to the task. In many ways she was regretting that she had agreed to creep away like this in the middle of the night. It would have been more honourable to have faced Shaun openly and told him that she was joining James. Yet in doing so, she would have been forced to disregard James' own demand for secrecy. She sighed. Caught between two choices, she had resolved neither to her own satisfaction.

'You come now.' Felipe was sounding agitated again..

Gabrielle groaned and got to her feet. She was sleepy, and she still hadn't got over her bout of fever, she thought rather resentfully.

'*Es lejos?* Is it far?' she asked.

He shrugged and muttered something in return, giving her a curious sidelong glance as if he was puzzled at something. They had been following a rough track before, but now this disappeared completely, and they seemed to be fighting their way through solid jungle. Felipe had to use his machete to cut them a path, and every swing he made with it was accompanied by a curse.

It was like a living nightmare, Gabrielle thought desperately as unseen obstructions caught at her clothing and hair, and thorns scratched at her arms and legs. Feathery fronds brushed across her face, and she had to bite her lip hard to stop herself from crying out. It was important somehow for Felipe not to see that she was afraid.

She had been aware that there was danger in this beautiful green wilderness since she had first set foot there, but until this moment she had always felt safe, she realised. Shaun's leadership of the expedition might have been abrasive, but it seemed to give everyone taking part a curious sense of security, even in the most insecure situations. He respected the forest, she thought, and took no unnecessary risks.

Now, for the first time, she had to face the possibility that she might die as other people had died of exhaustion and exposure, if not from snakebite or an attack from a wild animal. She swallowed the sudden bitterness in her mouth. After all, who would look for them? At Ixtlacan, Shaun would guess she had gone with Felipe and why. And if she did not get to James, he would probably assume she had refused to come.

She touched Felipe's arm. '*Estamos perdidos?*' she asked, trying to keep her voice steady.

He turned on her, his face vicious, biting out a flood of words whose meaning she was only able to guess at. One thing seemed clear—Felipe held her responsible for whatever trouble they were in. She would have found it ludicrous if she hadn't been so scared.

One thing was certain—they would achieve nothing and simply waste energy by blundering about in the darkness as they were doing. They had lost the trail completely, and she doubted their ability to find it again. She tried to remember some of the things that Anna had told her about the Ixtlacan region. Hadn't she said it lay between two rivers? They had travelled here on one of them—the Rio Torcido. She felt an inward chill as she remembered what the name meant. Perhaps it was cursed—perhaps the whole expedition had been cursed too, finding the site but losing the treasure it had contained.

The Mayan gods had demanded living sacrifice, a voice whispered inside her, and she squared her shoulders, fighting the thought. They wouldn't find a willing victim in her!

The more she considered the situation, the more convinced she felt that they should try and make their way to one of the rivers. She doubted whether there would be any settlements, but surely there would be *chicle* camps somewhere near the water?

It was not easy explaining all this to Felipe, whose reaction was sullen, but at least when she mentioned the word '*rio*' he seemed to know what she was talking about, and even to know the direction they should take. Their progress was still slow, and they stopped for frequent rests, but at last they seemed to have some sense of purpose. Felipe became slightly more cheerful and kept tapping his pack meaningfully. From the few slightly cryptic remarks that he let fall, Gabrielle gathered to her astonishment that the pack actually contained an inflatable rubber dinghy of some kind, and she guessed that he had stolen it from the Institute equipment. She groaned inwardly. This would be just another black mark against her as far as Shaun was concerned, she thought, and chided herself for her own foolishness. She would never see Shaun again, so it could make very little difference what his thoughts about her might be. A feeling of desolation spread over her at this realisation.

She looked at the illuminated dial of her watch and saw that there was only another hour before sunrise. They seemed to have been walking for ever, and her aching muscles were protesting at every new step. She could hardly believe it when at last her ears caught the distant noise of running water. They were approaching the river.

At first sight, when they emerged through the trees, it seemed even less prepossessing than the Rio Torcido. Gabrielle could see flecks of foam as it plunged over hidden rocks, and the idea of trying to negotiate these in a flimsy rubber boat frankly appalled her.

It did not seem to have much appeal for Felipe either, for he grudgingly announced that they would wait for sunrise before embarking.

Gabrielle rather limply found a tree with a conveniently low forked branch and scrambled up into it, lodging her pack behind her as a pillow. It was neither as safe nor as comfortable as her hammock back at the camp, but she managed to doze fitfully for a while.

When Felipe woke her, she found he had already inflated the boat. Its gay red and yellow colouring looked incongruous in the wilderness of the setting, and when Felipe launched it on the Rio, it looked pathetically small. It certainly did not seem of a size to accommodate two people, and Gabrielle suspected it had never been intended to carry a passenger. She watched Felipe uncertainly as he assembled the two lightweight oars it carried, then climbed obediently aboard with a good deal of inward trepidation.

The boats they had travelled in before had been of shallow draught, but they had felt considerably more secure than this. The water hissed and gurgled round the dinghy's fragile sides, and Gabrielle looked round for something to bale with. Felipe was pulling strongly on the oars, but he did not seem to be making much headway against the strength of the current. Gabrielle prayed silently that they would see some signs of life before long. She didn't trust the boat, nor Felipe's skill at handling it for very long in these conditions.

Felipe's own confidence too, seemed to be ebbing, she noticed. After a while, he rested on the oars and stared at her.

'Too heavy,' he announced. 'We carry too much.'

In other circumstances, Gabrielle would have asked sarcastically if he wanted her to swim behind, but she decided at the moment it was probably better to keep quiet. It never occurred to her what he might be getting at, until he made a lunge for the camera case at her feet.

'No!' Gabrielle grabbed for it too, instinctively, and the dinghy rocked terrifyingly.

'For God's sake, keep still! You'll drown us both!' she shouted at him, her face white.

He looked small and ugly. 'You crazy, *gringa*. You drown us. This'—he dragged the strap of the camera case out of her fingers with a force that made her cry out in pain—'this goes.'

The heavy case sank as soon as it hit the water, as if it had been sucked down some giant, hidden throat. Gabrielle felt physically ill as she watched it vanish. They were all insured, of course—the Hasselbladt that *Vision* had provided her with, as well as the ciné-camera and her own Pentax, but that was not the point. The Pentax had been the first decent camera she had ever possessed, the culmination of innumerable dreams and ambitions. It had taken time and sacrifice to enable her to buy it, and now it was gone for ever, at the bottom of some wild, nameless river, and no amount of insurance money would ever replace what it had meant to her, or the independence it had represented. She wanted, very badly, to cry, but she would not give Felipe that satisfaction. He looked at her, leering triumphantly.

'So,' he said. 'Now we get on, *gringa*.'

She did not speak, and they travelled for nearly half an hour in silence, making painfully slow progress. Although she scanned the neighbouring banks until her eyes ached, Gabrielle could see no other signs of life, not even a distant trail of smoke from a tell-tale camp fire.

It was getting hotter and hotter all the time, and Felipe began to mutter, before flinging down his paddle, and tearing off his jacket. His hair was hanging in his eyes, and his shirt was stained with sweat and sticking to him. He was an unattractive sight. As he went to retrieve his paddle, it happened. A sudden current seized the dinghy, dragging it sideways towards the bank. It was Gabrielle who saw the tree trunk first, its jagged branches half submerged in the water, but her warning scream came too late. The dinghy caught, tore and began to fill with water. There was no point in remaining in a sinking boat, Gabrielle thought desperately, as she plunged into the river and began to struggle against the powerful current towards the bank. The tree which had been their downfall now came to her aid. She grabbed some of the trailing branches and pulled herself towards the massive trunk, clinging to it while she regained her breath and some of her strength. For a moment she could see no sign of Felipe and just as she was wondering desperately if he had drowned, and if she was alone in the jungle, she caught sight of a bedraggled figure dragging itself out of the water on to the bank.

She crawled up on to the tree trunk and made her way unsteadily along it until she too reached dry land. Then she collapsed on the ground, her teeth chattering more with reaction than cold.

Her first coherent thought was that now they were in a bigger mess than ever. They'd lost their only means of transport, and with it, all their equipment. Even Felipe's machete was now at the bottom of the river. She shivered uncontrollably. The gods seemed determined on vengeance, she thought hysterically.

Felipe was sitting a few yards away, hugging himself and moaning. As she got up wearily and went over to him, he looked up with burning eyes and launched into another of his high-pitched and wholly incomprehensible tirades.

Her temper snapped. 'Well, don't blame me,' she blazed at him. 'You said you would take me to Don Jaime. So far you've got us lost and nearly drowned us. I don't think you even know where Don Jaime is.'

He stared up at her, silent and open-mouthed as if he had seen her suddenly go mad.

'But you know where he is, *gringa*. You can find Don Jaime.'

It was her turn to stare. 'I? I haven't the faintest idea how to find him. You said he wanted me. You brought me a message. You were going to take me to him ...' Her voice tailed away as Felipe's eyes shifted away from hers.

'No,' she whispered after a moment. 'It wasn't like that, was it? You wanted to find him, so you came to me and spun me a tale hoping that I'd take you there. You don't know where James is any more than I do.'

Felipe got to his feet in one snake-like movement. He reached for her hand—the bandaged hand, and she bit back a cry as his fingers closed round it.

'Don't play games, *gringa*, or someone gets hurt. You

take me to Don Jaime now. You know where, or why you come here? All the time people say you know where he is.'

'I don't know.' If he didn't stop squeezing her hand, she thought she would faint.

'I don't believe you, *gringa.* Why else you come to Merida? Why you look in his room?'

'Who told you that?' But even as she asked the question, she knew the answer. It was obvious that Felipe, whatever he was up to, had to have an accomplice at the Institute itself.

'Isabella's a very clever girl,' she went on quietly, noting the betraying flicker of his eyes at the mention of the girl's name, confirming that she had guessed correctly. 'But she hasn't been quite clever enough. I haven't been very clever either, or I would have remembered. Don Jaime never got my letters. He doesn't even know I'm in the Yucatan.'

'You lie,' Felipe said almost pleasantly, and slapped her hard across the face with his free hand.

She moistened her dry lips with her tongue. 'I'm not lying. I've no reason to lie to you. I came with you only because you made me think Don Jaime needed me, and you knew where he could be found.' She looked at him. 'Why do you want to find him, Felipe?'

He shook his head. 'You don't ask questions, *gringa.* You answer them,' he said, his voice emotionless, and Gabrielle was afraid.

She was certain, suddenly, that Felipe would kill her now that she was no use to him, and that even if he did not administer the *coup de grâce* himself, he would leave her here in the forest to die. There was nothing she could say or do to prevent him, either. She had nothing to bargain with. She had no doubt now that Felipe was connected with the *estoleros* and that this was why he was looking for James. One more death probably would not matter, she thought.

From the cover of the trees, Shaun Lennox said drily, 'I

think this has gone far enough, don't you?'

Pablo was with him, and she saw incredulously that they were both carrying guns. Felipe had gone a sallow, grey colour.

Shaun walked towards them, lowering the muzzle of his gun. He looked them over in silence, assimilating their drenched and mud-stained clothes.

'You choose strange rendezvous, Gabrielle,' he remarked. 'Even for a thieves' picnic.'

His words stung and she flushed.

'You must let me explain——' she began, but he cut her off abruptly.

'It's a little late for explanations. I gave you every chance—made every allowance. But as soon as this little rat showed up, you were off with him as soon as my back was turned—or at least when you thought it was turned. But I couldn't sleep either, Gabrielle. Do you suppose it can have been the moonlight keeping me awake? Whatever it was, I saw you sneaking off. Pablo and I haven't been far behind you all the time.'

The blaze of relief she had felt at seeing him was dying now in the chill of his words.

He went on in the same quiet tone. 'It has its amusing side, of course. You and Felipe here, following each other round in circles, each convinced the other one knows where James is. You should have asked me.'

'You—know?' Her breath escaped in a sigh of incredulity.

'I have a damn good idea,' he said grimly. 'We only just missed him at Ixtlacan, you know, so he can't be too far away.' He gestured towards Pablo. 'Tell the *señora, amigo.*'

Pablo's eyes were anxious. He said haltingly, 'There is a—*chicle* camp, *señora,* not far from *las ruinas*. No one goes there any more. It is a bad place. But when Francisco and I were there a few days since, someone had been using it. Not a *chiclero*—this man hid from us. *Chicleros* do not hide from their own.'

No, she thought, but a man who had stolen a treasure from a Mayan site and was trying to evade the *estoleros* would hide.

'Can you—show me where this place is?' She directed the question to Pablo, but she knew the answer would come from Shaun.

'Yes, he'll take you there, if that's what you want,' he said bleakly. 'Are you sure that it is?'

She wanted to tell him that she was sure of nothing any more. That every certainty she had ever possessed had been turned on its head, leaving her solitary and afraid, and that without the strength and reassurance of his arms around her and his lips on hers, she was nothing. But he was a stranger now, locked behind a barrier of contempt and indifference. He might still want her physically, but he despised her at the same time. If he had loved her, he would have known she was innocent of any involvement in James' schemes and known too why she had had to go with Felipe.

She couldn't look at him, though, and tell him these things and see the accusation and disbelief in his eyes again. That hurt too much. So she looked down at the floor, and said 'Yes' so quietly that he had to bend his head to catch the word.

She heard him give a quick, bitter sigh. 'Then we'll go now,' he said abruptly. 'Pablo reckons we can make it before nightfall.'

'What about—him?' Gabrielle still did not look up, but motioned with her hand in the direction of the now silent Felipe.

'He comes too. Later he can go back to Merida in the supply helicopter. The police are waiting for him, and the Guatemalan authorities are waiting to pick any pieces they leave.' He glanced round, his brows raised. 'I can see the necessity for travelling light, but didn't you bring anything in the way of gear?'

Tonelessly she explained how the boat had sunk, taking their packs with it.

'You're not the most successful fugitives in the history of the world. What about your other things—the cameras?'

'Felipe threw them out of the boat. He said they were too heavy.' To her horror she felt tears pricking at her eyes, and rubbed at them fiercely with her hand as a child might have done.

She heard Shaun mutter something under his breath, but when she looked up his face was like a mask, smooth and unreadable.

'That's unfortunate,' he said after a moment. 'There are some cameras back at base. They won't be as sophisticated as the ones you've been using, but I suppose they're better than nothing.'

He turned to Felipe and began speaking to him in Spanish. His tone sounded pleasant enough, but Gabrielle saw the other man cringe away as from a blow, his sallow face twisted with hate.

Shaun came back to her side and stood for a moment, his blue eyes searching her face.

'Are you ready?'

'Yes.'

Try as she would, there was a world of defeat in the monosyllable. Her hand was painful from the working over it had received from Felipe, and she was trembling violently inside.

'We need to make a move soon, if we're to get there before sunset. We have some pretty rough country to cover, Pablo says.' Shaun's voice took on a faintly jeering note. 'What's the matter, Gabrielle? Has the market in wifely devotion suffered a sudden recession?'

She winced. 'That's—cruel,' she whispered.

'I don't feel particularly gentle at the moment,' he said

roughly. 'I've known a lot of women in my time, Gabrielle, but you're something new in my experience—thank God. Your type isn't new, though. I think Byron had found someone just like you when he wrote "Thou false to him, Thou fiend to me".'

He swung away from her almost violently. She lifted her bandaged hand to her cheek and cradled it there, as if she was recovering from a physical blow. In a way, she thought dazedly, it would have been easier if he had struck her. Anything would have been better than this bitterness, this sense of total separation. Yet what right had she to expect anything else? As far as he was concerned, she was simply another man's wife.

They set out half an hour later. The slight delay had been caused by Pablo, who had discovered there were *machacha* fish in the river and produced a hook and line. Gabrielle was not impressed with the catch he gradually accumulated on the river bank. They were unattractive fish with large eyes and almost human-looking teeth, but Pablo assured her they were very good to eat, and she made no further demur, guessing that the amount of food that Shaun had brought with him was probably limited and the fish would be needed to supplement it.

They walked for nearly two hours before Shaun decided to allow time for a rest and a meal. Pablo built a small fire and cooked the fish on an improvised spit. In spite of its appearance and numerous bones, Gabrielle found the *machacha* flesh was thick and tasty and she ate with more appetite than she had believed she possessed.

She leaned back against the trunk of a tree and closed her eyes. It was good to be completely still in an atmosphere where the very slightest movement transformed her skin into a bath of perspiration. She had lost her hat in the river, and her hair clung in clammy tendrils round her face and neck.

Yet in some way the physical effort and its attendant discomforts were a relief. At least they occupied her mind to the exclusion of everything else. As soon as she relaxed, her personal problems came crowding back into her thoughts to torture her.

She felt a shadow fall across her and looked up to see Shaun.

'How's your hand?' he asked without preamble.

'It's fine,' she lied, resisting an impulse to hide it behind her.

'Let me see.' He knelt down at her side and before she could protest, began to unwind the grimy bandage. His lips compressed. 'You're asking for another infection,' he said grimly. 'Haven't we got enough on our plates without that?'

'I'm sorry.'

'Don't be.' His eyes studied her face for a moment, taking in the shadowed eyes, the skin drawn tautly over her high cheekbones, then he turned back to his task.

Gabrielle could sense the tension and anger in him, and marvelled how none of it was conveyed in the sure gentleness of his touch as he cleaned her hand and provided a fresh dressing for it. She looked down at his bent head and had to suppress an overwhelming longing to bury her face in the crisp dark hair where it grew down on his neck. Grimy he might be, unshaven he definitely was, but nothing could detract from the aura of sheer male attraction that was as much a part of him as his skin. The arrogant set of his shoulders, his firm mouth, every inch of his lean, muscular body proclaimed it.

It was frightening, this power that he had over her, frightening and a little shaming that her whole body could dissolve into melting longing at the merest brush of his hand.

As if he could divine her thoughts, he looked up suddenly into her face and she was sickeningly conscious of how she must look—enormous-eyed, her lips full and tremulous, and the faint flush of love-desire on her cheeks. Shaun released her hand as if he had been stung, but he did not get up and walk away as she had half expected. He remained kneeling, his face only a matter of inches from her own. She wanted to touch him, to feel the damp warmth of his skin under her fingers and the roughness of his cheek beneath her lips. Almost involuntarily, her back began to arch away from the tree trunk, forcing her body closer to his. He moved then, shaking his head almost helplessly as a groan of protest forced itself from his lips.

'What in hell do you want from me, Gabrielle?' he demanded in a savage undertone. 'I don't pretend to be a saint and my control has its limits. What do you want me to do—order Pablo and Felipe to turn their backs so I can tumble you here in the grass like a whore?'

'I want you to love me,' she said huskily. 'In however many ways there are, Shaun. I—I can't settle for anything less.'

His eyes flicked unwillingly from her quivering mouth to the roundness of her breasts, straining against the thin shirt.

'You sell yourself well.' His voice was quiet, but it fell across her jangling nerves like a whiplash. 'No wonder Warner was such an eager purchaser, poor bastard. But I'm not in the market—haven't I made that clear enough to you? Don't offer what you're not prepared to give.'

'I'll give,' she whispered. 'I'd give you anything ...'

'It isn't yours to give,' he said. 'Or had you forgotten?' He got to his feet, brushing grass and leaves from his pants with hands that were not entirely steady. When he spoke, his voice was brisk and remote. 'On your feet, Mrs Warner. We mustn't keep your husband waiting any longer.'

Humiliated tears blinded her, as he turned and strode away.

The mosquitoes attacked in droves during the afternoon. Gabrielle thought longingly of the tubes of insect repellent that she and Anna had used so liberally at the camp, but she was almost too exhausted to do more than go through the motions of brushing them away. Mentally and physically, she was numb, incapable of doing more than setting one weary foot in front of the other, indifferent to the sharp spines on the plants which ripped at her clothes and skin as she brushed past on the narrow trail.

Occasionally the trail petered out altogether, and she stood silent, her head bent, while Shaun and Pablo cleared a path with their machetes. Felipe stood a little apart, holding the packs, his eyes fixed on the gleaming machetes as if he had very different plans for their use. He seemed subdued, but something told Gabrielle that this was only a façade.

Pablo was the only cheerful member of the party, assuring them with eternal optimism, '*No es lejos*. It isn't far now.'

Gabrielle swallowed past a throat that felt as if it was coated in fur. What would happen if James wasn't there when they arrived? she thought drearily. She seemed to have been pursuing him eternally—first to Merida, then to the base camp and finally to Ixtlacan. Perhaps she was fated never to meet him. She shivered at the thought.

Just at that moment, the sun broke through the dense roof of foliage above her head, and she lifted her face to it gratefully, as if it was a good omen.

'Courage, *señora*.' Pablo spoke to her, his face puckered anxiously. 'Soon we shall reach the *arroyo*. There you may call to your husband if you wish, and he will be able to hear you.'

She tried to smile at him, but the words of thanks she was formulating died on her lips at a sudden new sound which assailed their ears. It was a loud guttural roar, coming from the thicket of vines and thorns on their right and less than a hundred yards away.

A wail burst from Felipe. *'El tigre!'* he shouted, his eyes bulging in his sweat-streaked face. Before any of them could move, he threw down the pack he was carrying and bolted into the jungle. Pablo cursed and lifted his gun to his shoulder, but a word from Shaun and he froze into immobility, his finger relaxing from the trigger. They exchanged a few words, then Pablo heaved the discarded pack on to his own shoulders and they made to set off again.

Gabrielle caught at Shaun's arm. 'You're letting him go?'

He looked down at her coldly. 'What do you expect me to do—run after him?'

'But you said the police wanted him ...'

'So they do—but Felipe prefers to take his chance in the jungle. It's his decision.'

'But he'll get away.'

'Will he?' His face was wry. 'He'll run until he drops and what then? He has no food, no weapons—nothing. I think he might have found a prison sentence easier.'

She stared at his implacable face, then turned to Pablo, who shrugged and crossed himself.

'Maybe he lives, maybe he dies, *señora.* Who can tell? *La selva es asi*—the jungle is like that.'

'And that roar?' she asked shakily. 'Was it really a *tigre* —a jaguar? Will it attack us?'

Pablo roared with laughter, and even Shaun accorded her a reluctant smile.

'It was no jaguar,' he said. 'It was a *saraguate*—a big ape. It imitates the jaguar's roar to keep intruders away. It probably has females to protect. It's warned us, and we'll respect that warning and keep out of its way.'

She flushed, feeling foolish. Pablo gave her shoulder an encouraging pat.

'You have courage, *señora*,' he approved. 'You did not run like that *loco* Felipe.'

Gabrielle did not spoil the effect by telling him that it had only been because she did not think her legs would carry her, and summoned a weak smile.

They had all slowed to almost a snail's pace when they saw the *arroyo* sparkling through the trees. Gabrielle knelt down on the bank and lifted handfuls of water to splash on her face, trickling it liberally down the neck of her shirt. Ahead of them she could see that the trail widened considerably leading to a large clearing.

'Well, go on.' Shaun's voice was hard. 'You heard what Pablo said. If you call to Warner from here, he'll be able to hear you. Perhaps you can persuade him not to go into hiding again.'

She lifted her canteen to her mouth and rinsed her throat carefully.

'James!' she shouted. 'It's me—it's Gabrielle! I'm down by the *arroyo*. Dr Lennox is with me. We're—we're coming into the camp. James, don't do anything silly.'

She paused. Shaun stood, his head bent, listening intently, but no sound came back through the trees. There was a total, almost frightening silence.

She tried again. 'James, I know it must be a shock for you, but it's for the best. We can't go on like this . . .'

Her voice stopped helplessly of its own accord, but she met with no response.

She turned to Shaun appealingly, but his face was grim and set.

'We go in,' he said briefly, and shouldered his rifle.

They crossed the *arroyo* and trod warily down the trail to the camp. Monkeys, apparently frightened by the sound of the human voice, began chattering again in the neighbouring trees.

Gabrielle felt sick with apprehension as they emerged into the clearing. It had a desolate air. Several *champas* had been constructed there, but the palm roofs were torn and ragged, and the supporting poles leaned drunkenly. One of them, however, was in slightly better condition than the rest, and in this someone had slung a hammock. Even across the clearing Gabrielle could see it was occupied, and as she watched, one hand pressed to her mouth, it moved slightly.

She forced her weary legs to a shambling run across the tussocky grass, aware that Shaun and Pablo were keeping pace with her, but by some superhuman effort she reached the *champa* first.

A man lay in the hammock, a gaunt, emaciated figure, eyes bright with fever. There was a nauseous smell of dirt and vomit, and a faint sickly sweet odour that she could not recognise.

She forced herself to lay her fingers over the burning hand on top of the soiled sleeping bag.

'James?' she whispered disbelievingly.

The cracked lips opened, and the wild eyes seemed to focus on her for a moment.

'Who—are you?' he muttered.

CHAPTER EIGHT

GABRIELLE stood perfectly still, her head reeling wildly. This was the supreme irony, she thought. After all the miles she had travelled, the discomforts she had borne and the dangers, not to mention the mental agonies she had been through, and now James did not even recognise her. She felt a laugh bubbling up inside her and checked it fiercely, realising she was on the verge of hysteria.

Then Shaun's arm was at her waist, hard and muscular, forcing her to stay upright, to straighten her back and lift her tired shoulders.

'Hullo, Warner.' His face was grave as he looked down at the older man. 'It's been a long time.'

For a moment the glazed, unknowing look left James Warner's eyes and they sharpened intelligently.

'Lennox?' The harsh whisper, so unlike James' usually well-modulated tone, grated on Gabrielle's ears. 'What—are you doing here?'

'I came to find you.' Shaun's voice was calm, almost gentle.

'But—not just—me, eh?' Her husband's gaunt body shook convulsively for a moment and Gabrielle realised with a sense of shock that he was trying to laugh.

'No,' Shaun conceded. His eyes studied James' emaciated frame, lingering frowningly over his right leg, encased in a rough bloodstained bandage. 'What happened? Did your—friends decide to play rough?'

'They were—ungrateful,' the sick man muttered. 'All I'd done for them—forgotten—quite forgotten. They didn't want the stelae—this time. Too much time, they said. Too much trouble. They wanted the—things from the tomb, instead.'

'But you were too clever for them?'

'Yes.' James Warner lay back, his head beaded with sweat as if his previous long speech had deprived him of strength. His eyes were closed, and his breathing was shallow and noisy.

Shaun turned to Gabrielle. 'Go and get the medical kit from the pack,' he said tersely. 'Bring it to me here, then help Pablo build a fire. I need some water heating first, and then you can try and concoct some kind of meal for him. There's some dried soup powder, I think.'

She lingered, her eyes going apprehensively over the unresponsive figure in the hammock. 'What's the matter with him?' she whispered.

His lips twisted. 'Fetch the medical kit and I'll try to find out. At first glance I would say someone had shot him in the leg. Now hurry, for God's sake!'

He bent over James' recumbent figure and began to loosen the filthy bandage. Gabrielle turned away, glad of her errand. In spite of her concern, she knew that the next few minutes were likely to be nauseating.

If only there was some air she could breathe, she thought, gulping. Pablo took her arm, his grip comforting.

'Sit down, *señora.* I will fetch what is needed. Put your head down—so. You will be better soon.'

She obeyed him, tears of weakness pricking at her eyelids, thankful when the terrifying feeling of faintness began to pass. Pablo busied himself collecting wood for the fire and Gabrielle searched for the dried soup Shaun had described. Preparing the soup was the sort of mindless task she needed.

'That smells better than it looks,' Shaun remarked from behind her, and she jumped slightly. 'I hope you've made enough for all of us.'

'I think so—although guessing the quantities was rather difficult.' What nonsense was this she was talking? she asked herself wildly. How could she chat inconsequentially about—culinary difficulties while her husband lay only a few yards away, a self-confessed thief, shot by his own accomplices? 'The only thing is—James hates bought soups, both the packet and tinned variety.'

'I shouldn't worry about that.' He picked up a tin bowl and began to ladle some of the soup into it. 'I think you'll find that the prospect of starvation has an amazingly humanising effect on the taste buds.' He lifted his eyebrows at her enquiringly. 'Will you feed him, or shall I?'

'I will.' She held out her hand for the bowl, and he passed it to her, with a faint, twisted smile.

'Salving your guilty conscience, Gabrielle?' The words were mocking, but there was something else, just below the surface.

'Perhaps,' she told him levelly. But if she was, she thought as she carried the soup towards the *champa*, then it was not for the reason that he imagined. Her only guilt lay in the fact that she felt no more for James than the pity she would have experienced for a complete stranger under the same circumstances. His failure even to recognise her had not hurt her, because it was merely the confirmation of everything she had suspected about their relationship. Their marriage had never existed, except in the terms of a legal formality.

James looked slightly better than when she had last seen him. The soiled and stinking clothes and sleeping bag had been removed, and he was wrapped in one of Shaun's shirts. He had been washed too, and his leg had been freshly bandaged.

She knelt down awkwardly, taking care not to spill the soup.

'James,' she said softly, 'I've brought you something to eat. Have some of it while it's hot.'

His eyes opened slowly, wandering over her with detached interest.

'You're—very kind.' There was not a flicker of recognition in his eyes or in his polite voice. He allowed her to spoon the soup into his mouth, a little at a time, wiping away the residue that trickled down his chin with a clean handkerchief. This, she thought, was the most unnerving thing of all—James, the fastidious, the independent who had always kept her at arm's length, being reduced to this sort of dependence.

When about half the bowl's contents had gone, he turned his head away weakly. 'No more, thank you.'

On an impulse she laid her left hand, the one that wore his ring, over his. 'James . . .'

He looked at her, his eyes puzzled and a little remote.

'Do—I know you?' Her familiarity in using his Christian name obviously disturbed him, she realised.

'I'm sorry, Dr Warner.' She stood up. 'You—don't remember me, do you?'

'Should I?' His forehead puckered wearily as he looked up at her. 'I suppose you—must be—Lennox' wife.'

'No.' She swallowed past the sudden painful lump in her throat. 'I—I just work at the Institute.'

She turned and walked back to the fire. It was dark now, and the flames were friendly and reassuring. She sat down, gratefully accepting the purely physical comfort of its warmth, and Pablo handed her a bowl of soup. Shaun had been right, she thought after a few mouthfuls. It both smelled and tasted better than it looked, and she ate with an appetite she had not realised she possessed.

'Feeling better?' Shaun was standing beside her.

'Yes. And James ate nearly half of his.'

'That's fine.' She knew she had not imagined the hesitation in his voice, odd in one usually so forthright. She looked up at him, shading her face from the firelight with her hand.

'What is it?' she asked.

'He's a very sick man, Gabrielle.'

'Yes,' she said quickly. 'I was thinking, Shaun. Have

we any way of contacting the supply helicopter? It could land here, surely, and we could get James to hospital.'

He looked at her for a minute, then shook his head slowly.

'You—can't contact anyone?' she queried.

'I could. I have some signal flares in the pack.'

'But you're not going to use them,' she said almost incredulously. 'Shaun, you must. No matter what James has done, you can't let him suffer needlessly.'

His eyes were dark with anger. 'Do you really think I'm capable of that?' he demanded.

'No.' Ashamed, she hung her head, her voice almost inaudible. 'But he needs expert help, you must see that.'

'He needed it, yes,' he said quietly, and for a moment the significance of his words, the tense he had used escaped her. When realisation came, she flung up her head and looked at him, her heart pounding.

'It's not true! He—he's better. Anyone can see that.'

'Anyone who sees that is a fool.' He squatted down beside her, taking both her hands in his. 'He was shot days ago, Gabrielle. The bullet has never been removed from his leg, or the wound treated properly. It's become gangrenous. Didn't you realise?'

'But if we get him to hospital, surely they could do something—operate. It's just possible, isn't it?'

His clasp on her hands tightened. 'If I thought it would help you, I'd say yes. But it's pointless, Gabrielle. James hasn't got—time for that any more. He'd never make it to the hospital. It's even dubious whether he'd last until the helicopter got here.'

She sat rigid, the last vestige of colour draining from her face. She had wanted to be free, longed to be done with this pathetic farce of a marriage, but not at this cost—a man's life.

Shaun was speaking again. 'I've made him as comfortable

as I can, but there's nothing more I can do for him. At least he won't be alone—when it happens.'

She thought, James has always been alone.

His voice became brusque. 'We only have two hammocks, so you can have mine. I'll stay near Warner in case he needs anything.'

'No.' She looked at him with determination. 'I'll sit up with him for part of the night at least. It's my right,' she added with finality, and saw his mouth snap shut on the protest she expected.

'As you wish,' he said coldly. 'You can get some rest first—I insist on that much. I'll wake you later.'

'You promise?' she said urgently. 'You won't just let me sleep on?'

He gave her a brief, wintry smile. 'I promise.'

She hesitated, painfully aware of what he must be thinking. She wanted to tell him how it really was, how she had to assuage her self-reproach at the failure of her marriage by performing the services for James when he was sick that he would never have permitted if he had been well. 'Shaun . . .'

'Oh, God, you don't have to explain,' he said with a kind of controlled violence. 'You're his wife. I don't need to know anything else. Now go and get some sleep. You'll need it.'

Her weary body slumped gratefully into the sparse comfort of the hammock, but sleep eluded her. There was no sleeping bag and she guessed Shaun must have taken it for James. The only coverlet she had was the poncho she had seen Shaun wearing on the river trip, and she drew its folds closely round her body. A faint breath of the cologne he used, and the sharper acrid smell of cigar smoke still hung about it, and she buried her face in the cloth for a moment, savouring them. At best, it was only a poor substitute for the arms of the man who had worn it, she told herself, then stopped with a feeling of self-loathing. It was wrong to feel like that, she thought despairingly. What kind of woman was she to be harbouring those kind of thoughts when her husband lay at death's door only a few yards away?

From where she lay, she could see the moon rising over the trees. The goddess Ixchel, cruel, wanton and faithless under her serene exterior. She could almost see that beautiful, primitive face twisted in a snarl of satisfaction as her victim's body arched for death at her feet, hear the whistle of the knife as it descended.

The dark figure of the priest loomed over her, and she cried out in terror as his hand came down on her.

'Easy, now.' Shaun's voice came to her from the darkness. 'You did insist that I woke you.'

'I was dreaming.' Fully conscious now, Gabrielle sat up, biting back a shudder at the remembrance of that dream. Her eyes widened as she studied the illuminated dial of her wrist watch. 'But the night's nearly over . . .'

'Don't worry—I haven't cheated you of your wifely duty. Pablo took a turn as well.'

'I see. That was—good of him.' She pushed aside the entangling folds of the poncho and swung her legs over the side of the hammock. 'How is James now?'

'He seems fairly lucid at the moment.' He paused. 'He's asked for you.'

She was fastening her shoes, and her hands began to shake so much that she could not go on.

'Here, let me,' he said impatiently.

'What did he say?' she asked in a low voice, looking down at his bent head.

He shrugged, not looking at her. 'He said, "My wife—I want my wife." I was about to fetch you anyway.'

'Yes,' she said, dry-throated. 'Thank you.'

'De nada.' He stood up, his whole attitude impersonal and somehow forbidding. She knew he was watching her, as she crossed the clearing and walked into James' *champa.*

He was tossing restlessly and she bent over him, alarmed. His eyes focussed on her with difficulty. 'Want—my wife,' he gasped.

'Yes.' She took his hand, noticing with concern how burning hot he seemed again. 'I'm here, James. Don't worry any more.'

But her presence did not seem to bring him the reassurance he sought. He became more restless, struggling feebly against all her efforts to calm him and make him comfortable. At last he lay quietly, and she relaxed for a moment before she became aware that he was talking.

'Jade——' the word came clearly to her ears. 'Jade—beautiful jade. Now I'll show them. They won't pass me over any more.'

Gabrielle bent over him with sudden urgency. 'James, what jade are you talking about?'

'Jade—from the tomb. The—priest of—Ixchel. His—mask. So beautiful. I—found it. When she sees it—she'll know. She'll—understand why I had to go away.'

'I understand,' she said with difficulty. 'Don't talk now, James. Try to rest.'

She put her hand on his, trying to soothe him, and he seized it in a grip that hurt.

'I'll give it to you.' His voice was laboured and hoarse. 'Jade—like your eyes. I'll give you anything, if you promise you won't go—won't leave me.'

'I won't leave,' she said, desperately trying to free her hand from his almost paralysing grip. 'Go to sleep, James, and I'll be here when you wake up, I promise.'

'Tried—so hard.' His voice struggled on. 'Tried to—give you—everything—to make you stay. Had to get—money somehow. So young—so beautiful—eyes like jade. But—you always wanted—more.'

'No, James.' She was horrified. 'You can't have thought that! Whatever did I do . . .?'

The stumbling voice went on inexorably. 'You took—

everything. But nothing was ever—enough. That was why—I started to—take things from the sites. I—had to have—more money—had to get a bigger flat—give you the things you wanted—or you wouldn't stay. You told me you wouldn't—however much I begged . . .'

Gabrielle crossed her arms across her breasts as if she was defending herself from a blow. 'It isn't true,' she whispered. 'It isn't true. I didn't—I couldn't have . . .'

'You made me do it.' The cracked voice rose almost to a shout. 'It was for you—all for you.'

'What in the name of hell's going on?' Shaun pushed her to one side. His eyes lashed Gabrielle. 'What have you been saying to him? You've ruined his life, can't you even let the poor devil die in peace?'

She gave a choking cry and ran out of the sheltering *champa*. A storm of tears possessed her before she had taken more than a few stumbling steps on the uneven ground, and she threw herself down uncaring of bruises, digging her fingers into the yielding earth as if it was flesh.

She sensed he was beside her before the hard strength of his arms went round her, pulling her up, cradling her roughly against his body. In the shadows cast by the flickering fire, the sharp angles and planes of his face were more harshly defined than ever. His eyes were grim and angry when they met hers.

'It's a bit late for remorse, isn't it?' he bit at her.

'It's not true.' A sob came up into her throat, threatening to choke her.

'He thinks it is,' he said coldly. 'And he wasn't delirious when he told me the same story in Villahermosa.'

She stared at him incredulously. 'But I never said anything to him . . .'

'Perhaps you didn't have to. He's a middle-aged man married to a girl years younger than he is—a girl any man would want. Is it any wonder he was sick with terror at the thought you might leave him—that he tried to buy your —fidelity?'

She shook her head, burying her face in her hands.

'He didn't have to do that,' she said exhaustedly. 'I married him in good faith. I wanted to be a proper wife, but he didn't want that. He treated me as if I was something out of his collection—as if the flat where we lived was a glass case built especially for me.'

His hand came under her chin, brutally forcing up her face to meet his gaze.

'You said you wanted to be "a proper wife"—does that mean that your relationship was different from normal?'

She nodded unwillingly, feeling the warm blood forcing its way into her cheeks.

Shaun drew a sharp breath. 'You must put a high price on your favours,' he said harshly, and saw her wince.

After a moment she said in a low voice, 'What did he tell you in Villahermosa? You said you'd quarrelled—about me . . .'

'Oh, yes, we quarrelled,' he said grimly. 'Because I dared to suggest that no woman was worth what he'd done. He'd sacrificed his integrity and his scholarship, sold out the Institute time and time again—and for what? To keep you in luxury. He knew damned well he was under suspicion and had been for a couple of years, but he didn't stop, even though he knew that once we had proof it was the end of his career, and that he might even end up in jail.' He shook his head slowly. 'And he didn't even care.'

Gabrielle was silent. Her brain refused to accept the reality of this wild extravagant passion. She tried to look back calmly and detachedly over her brief married life with James—his coldness, his reserve, his apparent dislike of the most fleeting physical contact. She had often asked herself if he possessed even a scrap of ordinary affection or liking for her.

To learn that he had sacrificed his whole life in order to

keep her supplied with a standard of living she had never desired almost defeated her.

'I didn't even think he was fond of me,' she said almost inaudibly. 'If he'd just given me some sign . . .'

'He was afraid to—afraid that he wouldn't be able to control his feelings, and that he would disgust you. He was very conscious of the difference in your ages.' The contempt returned to his voice. 'He told me that he'd become aware very early in your relationship that you found physical lovemaking "distasteful".' He gave a brief, mirthless laugh. 'You can thank whatever god—or goddess—you choose that at least he'll never know the truth about you.'

'And what is the truth about me?' she asked quietly. 'Are you sure that you know it?'

'There are a lot of hard names for women like you,' he said. 'I don't propose to recite them now. I'll spare you that. But Warner was a fool not to have seen through you and your frigid maiden act. He should have knocked you off that pedestal and taken you to bed. Then at least he might have felt he'd had his money's worth.'

She lifted her arm and struck him across the face with all the force she was capable of. For an endless moment, they stared at each other, then Shaun turned on his heel and walked away.

In spite of the relative shade provided by the *champa*, it was stiflingly hot. Gabrielle sat beside James' hammock, watching him sleep. Pablo had improvised a rough fan of palm leaves and she was using this to keep the flies away from his recumbent body. He was sinking fast. It was obvious now from the strange transparency of his face and hands. Apart from short periods during the day when he had been restless with pain, he seemed to have spent most of the time in a shallow coma.

She had prepared the last of the soup for him, but he

had knocked the spoon weakly aside, and was subsisting on occasional sips of water.

Watching him, Gabrielle thought she had never felt so utterly helpless in her life. It was frightening how dependent one was on the trappings of civilisation, particularly where sickness and death were concerned. At home in England, there would have been the reassurance of a hospital ward, the skill of nurses as well as the immediate panacea of pain-killing injections and drugs. Here, all the comfort she could offer was the draught from a palm leaf fan, and a handkerchief wrung out in cool water to wipe his face with.

She heard a footstep beside her and turned to see Pablo, his face puckered with concern.

'How is the *señor*?' he whispered.

She lifted her shoulders wearily under the constricting shirt. 'As you see.'

He shook his head silently and crossed himself. 'I will sit with him if the *señora* wishes to bathe in the *arroyo*,' he offered after a while.

'No—thank you anyway, Pablo,' she said awkwardly. She could not explain that she was waiting here quite hopelessly for James to give some word, some sign that would vindicate her. She did not know how she was going to face the rest of her life, weighted down by the accusation that her greed had driven him to shame and death.

She saw that Pablo had left his gun propped at the entrance to the *champa*, and guessed he had been hunting.

'No sign of Felipe?' she asked.

'That evil one! If God is good, *señora*, he will have been meat for *el tigre* long since.'

Gabrielle shuddered at the picture his words conjured up.

'Pablo,' she began again after a pause, 'if Felipe was so evil, as you say, why did Señor Lennox allow him to go with us to Ixtlacan?'

Pablo shuffled uncomfortably. 'Felipe was guide—but not good one, *señora.* Yet always plenty money. People wonder how he gets all this money.'

'Presumably because he was working for the *estoleros.*'

Pablo nodded. '*Si, señora.* All the world knows this, but no one can get proof. Then Don Jaime goes into the forest with Felipe and long time after, Felipe comes back alone. Very angry. Drinks much, says foolish things. When we go to *las ruinas*, Felipe say he come too—as guide.' Pablo turned away and spat with great accuracy. 'So Señor Lennox agree. That way, maybe we find Don Jaime.'

'Because Señor Lennox thought that I knew where he was all the time, and that I would lead you to him?'

Pablo avoided her gaze. 'Maybe, *señora.* I don't know. All he tells me is that I should watch Felipe all the time, and I see him talk to you, *señora*, when no one else is near.'

Gabrielle sighed. 'Did Felipe shoot the *señor*?'

He looked at her in frank amazement. 'That one? He is only fit to hurt women and children, *señora.*'

She winced, recalling the pain Felipe had enjoyed inflicting on her injured hand. 'Then who did shoot him?'

'The *estoleros, señora.* Felipe was never one of them. He was—how you say . . .'

'A go-between?' she supplied, and he nodded.

'I think the *estoleros* are angry with Don Jaime because he does not give them the treasure from the tomb—and maybe they are angry with Felipe too, and so he tries hard to find Don Jaime so he can give him back to them.'

A thought had occurred to Gabrielle. 'But if Don Jaime ran away from the *estoleros* and they are still looking for him, that means he brought the treasure from the tomb with him.'

'*Si, señora,*' Pablo nodded eagerly. 'Señor Lennox searches and I search, but we not find. Only Don Jaime can tell now, and the good God knows whether he will ever speak again.' He looked down sombrely at James' motionless body as he spoke.

When he had gone, Gabrielle sat quietly wielding the fan in long, slow sweeps which sent trickles of sweat trickling down between her shoulder blades. Somewhere, possibly quite near at hand, were the jade mask and the other treasures from Ixtlacan, and somehow she had to discover where they were.

James stirred suddenly, his face constricted by a spasm of pain. He muttered something and his eyes opened, gazing round uncomprehendingly. She bent over him.

'James,' she whispered urgently.

The clouded eyes settled on her face. 'Who *are* you?' His voice was fretful and so weak she could barely catch the words.

'I'm your wife, James,' she told him steadily. 'You took some jade from a temple for me. You said it matched my eyes. But you haven't given it to me. You haven't even told me where it is.'

'Jade?' The word was hardly more than a sigh.

'Yes.' She moistened dry lips with her tongue. 'Please may I see it? You said it was for me—so that I would stay with you. Well, I'm here. I'll never leave you.'

'Never—leave—me.' A ghost of a smile appeared. 'My—lovely Elaine.'

Gabrielle sat as if she had been turned to stone. His first wife, she thought wildly, and with the realisation came an immense relief.

She put her hand over his. 'Yes,' she said, 'I'm Elaine.'

'The jade is—for you—Elaine. I didn't want—anyone else—to have it. I buried it—on the edge of the clearing. I marked—the place with stones—a letter E.'

His eyes closed as if the effort had been too much for him, and he relapsed into unconsciousness again. Gabrielle sat for a while, staring into space, then got to her feet stretching her cramped limbs.

Pablo was sitting not far from the *champa*, plucking the feathers from a wild pheasant which he held up triumphantly for her to see. She forced a smile in return. 'I'm going for a walk,' she told him. 'Please call me if Don Jaime wakes again.'

Pablo nodded and returned to his task. She walked to the edge of the clearing and circled it once, slowly, her eyes fixed to the ground, searching for the cairn of stones James had described. But her efforts were unsuccessful, and she began to wonder if the whole thing was not merely a sick man's fantasy. Perhaps James, wounded and a fugitive, had simply dropped the jade and other things in the forest during his flight. Then her foot struck against a stone, half concealed by a tangle of vines, and she tensed, kneeling to pull the creepers away. The dark earth had been disturbed recently, and stones had been piled there, although the rains had probably dislodged them from the original pattern. She piled them at the side, then began to dig in the ground with her bare hands. Presumably James had used the same implements, because the hole was only a shallow one. She dragged out the muddy package in its polythene covering, and knelt looking down at it.

'Gabrielle!' It was Shaun's voice, sharp with urgency. He was standing at the entrance to James' *champa* and as she looked at him, he lifted his arm to beckon her.

He did not have to tell her. She knew. She went into the *champa* and looked down at the still figure in the hammock. Pablo was standing, twisting his hat through nervous fingers.

'It was very quick, *señora*. Señor Lennox came to give him some water, and Don Jaime cried out just once, and died.'

'He's at peace now,' she said dully. She turned to Shaun, mutely holding out the package.

'He told you where it was?' He took it from her, turning it over in his hands almost disbelievingly.

She nodded tiredly. Reaction was setting in from the last few days, and she felt numb and sick.

'So that I would stay with him.' Her voice sounded strange in her own ears. 'And then I left him to go and find it. I didn't think it would be so soon, or I wouldn't have left him. I promised I wouldn't leave him!'

Someone far away was screaming these things, and Gabrielle wished that she would be quiet, so that she could lie down somewhere and sleep. A stinging slap across the cheek brought her back to reality. She stared at Shaun, shocked, her hand lifted protectively to her face.

'I'm sorry,' his voice was hard, 'but we haven't time for hysterics. Our major concern now is to give James a decent burial and get back to Ixtlacan before any unwelcome visitors decide to pay us a visit.' He looked at her white face and his tone softened slightly. 'I'm sorry we can't give him a conventional funeral.'

'I don't think he would have wanted that,' she said tonelessly. 'He loved the rain forest. I think he would possibly have chosen to be buried here.'

'Maybe he would at that,' he said quietly.

She went out into the open and sat down, with her back to a tree. Presently Pablo brought her a mug of coffee, black and bitter, and she drank it thirstily as if it was nectar. She noticed incuriously that heavy clouds were gathering, blotting out the sun. It would rain soon. She ran her hand round the back of her neck, lifting her hair away.

She had never known what it was to be a wife, and now she was a widow. She could not mourn for James in the conventional sense. In view of their relationship, that would be hypocritical. But there might be a time when she could grieve for other things—for the wasted months of their marriage, and for the obsession which had driven a clever, dedicated man to disgrace. She realised now that she had never known James at all, that the man she had married had been a stranger probably even to himself. The real James Warner had died a long time ago. It was only his shell that would lie in this scooped-out grave in the forest.

One day too, she thought, it might hurt that she had been chosen simply because she bore a superficial physical resemblance to a woman she had never met. Perhaps at first James had really thought she was Elaine, his first wife, come back to him. She sighed. He must have been speedily disillusioned.

That odd sense of detachment had returned, and with it came the rain with a soft pattering of drops that soon developed into a downpour. She lifted her face to it gratefully, relishing the coolness on her skin.

Somewhere in the distance she could hear Shaun calling to her, telling her to take shelter, but it was too much trouble to get up. Her limbs felt lethargic and would not obey her. How dark the clouds were! They seemed to press down on her.

He was beside her now. She could see that he was gripping her arm, shaking her, but oddly she could feel nothing. His lips were moving, but she did not recognise the words, and this distressed her because he looked so anxious. She had to reassure him somehow.

'My name is Elaine,' she informed him politely, and then the darkness swallowed her.

CHAPTER NINE

'I THINK I'd better come with you,' Aunt Molly said decisively.

'No.' Gabrielle shook her head. 'I have to stand on my own feet some time. You've been wonderful, and you mustn't think I don't appreciate all you've done for me. But I really feel this is something I've got to face alone.'

'They don't give you much warning.' Aunt Molly picked up the letter which had arrived that morning and studied it.

'Well, it wasn't entirely unexpected,' Gabrielle returned drily.

'But won't it upset you—having to go back to the flat?'

'I don't think so. And the sooner all the things are packed up and sent to the Institute, the sooner I can see about letting the flat. It's just being wasted as it is.'

'You won't have to pack all the things yourself.'

'No. That's why I wrote to the Institute in London. They're sending an expert round to see exactly what there is. They'll arrange to have it all crated when the time comes.' Gabrielle smiled across the breakfast table at her aunt. 'Don't look so worried,' she urged. 'I feel fine again. The doctor was right—a complete rest was all I needed.'

'Hmm.' Aunt Molly was obviously unconvinced. 'You didn't see yourself when I collected you from Heathrow. You were like some sort of—zombie.'

'Well,' Gabrielle laughed, 'I'm far from being a zombie now. And I have to open the flat up again some time,' she added more quietly. 'This is the sort of incentive I need. If I hurry, I can catch the ten a.m. train, and that will give me time to get some of the dust-sheets off the furniture before this man arrives.'

She went out of the dining room and up the stairs to her room to fetch her coat and some outdoor shoes. It was a bright day for January, the streets and gardens rimed with frost, and the prospect of a trip to London was not a wholly unattractive one.

Although she had spoken so bravely to Aunt Molly, Gabrielle did not relish the thought of entering the flat again. Her aunt had arranged the details of Mrs Hutchinson's notice, and the shutting up of the flat in the first place. She had been wonderful, interviewing James' solicitors and obtaining confirmation of his death from the Mexican authorities. His will had been a simple one, made a few days before their marriage and leaving everything to Gabrielle. There had not been a great deal of money after all, but there was his collection, and as soon as Gabrielle felt well enough to start coping with her own affairs again, she had written to the Institute's London headquarters outlining the position frankly, and asking them to make arrangements to dispose of the collection as they thought fit.

Knowing the usually slow workings of any kind of bureau, she had not expected a speedy reply. But a letter had come almost by return of post, telling her that one of their experts would be pleased to meet her at the flat at eleven o'clock that morning.

Gabrielle supposed drily that they must be more than keen to have their missing treasures returned without delay.

She slipped on her dark brown suede coat, casting a critical glance at herself in the long mirror of her wardrobe. She was still too thin, her cheekbones too prominent and the hollows of her throat too pronounced. But at least she felt alive again. That dreadful emotional deadness had left her, and she no longer viewed the world as if it stood at the end of a dark and frightening tunnel.

Her memories of those last days in the Yucatan were fleeting and blurred. Anna's worried face hanging over her was one of the few vivid recollections—that and the temple of Ixchel, squat and black against the setting sun. She knew vaguely that she had been flown back to Merida in the supply helicopter, and she could recall waking up in a hospital bed with Mrs Morgan sitting beside her. But she didn't know when or how the decision had been made to fly her back to England. She had slept for most of the journey, hardly aware of Mrs Morgan who had accompanied her. The poor woman must have been thankful to have delivered her safely to Aunt Molly, Gabrielle thought wryly.

She fastened the zips on her matching suede boots and picked up her handbag. As she went downstairs, she saw Aunt Molly hovering rather anxiously in the hall.

'My dear, are you sure . . .'

'Quite sure.' Gabrielle kissed her on the cheek. 'I'm quite well again. Even Dr Forrest said I could start thinking about finding another job whenever I liked.'

'Have you told Dr Forrest how badly you're sleeping still?' her aunt retorted grimly. 'I thought not.' She shook her head in irritation. 'I just hope and pray that this visit to the flat doesn't revive a whole lot of memories that are best forgotten, that's all.'

It was a pleasant train ride, through bare woods, crowding with silver birches. It was all in marked contrast to what she had left behind in Mexico, Gabrielle thought as she stared out of the window.

She had never told her aunt, or the doctor either, the real reason for her disturbed nights or continuing pallor. Unless she talked in her sleep, Shaun's name had never crossed her lips since she had returned to England. Thoughts of him were inevitable, and the pain they engendered had been one of the first emotional responses she had been capable of.

She had told herself a hundred times she was a fool to expend so much thought and longing on a man who despised her. But at the same time she had to admit that the evidence against her had seemed overwhelming. She had almost managed to convince herself that she might be guilty in some unwitting way. There had been so many things to condemn her—her initial secrecy about the existence of her marriage and later, her association with Felipe. It was all so painfully clear now why no one had mentioned James to her. Either she was innocent of the whole affair or in collaboration with him, they must have reasoned, and until they were sure, silence must have seemed the safest option.

She suppressed a bitter little sigh. The result had been that she had been tried and condemned without being able to say a virtual word in her own defence. She tried to tell herself yet again that if Shaun had possessed any deeper feeling for her than a fleeting desire brought on by proximity, then he would have had more faith in her. But in her heart she doubted the truth of this. After all, James hadn't lied to him. He'd told him what he believed to be the truth, and the strain and confusion of his position must have brought him near breaking point. Shaun had known him and probably respected him for years, whereas she was a stranger to him, an unknown quality, no matter how physically attractive he might have found her.

She wished with all her heart that they need not have parted in such an atmosphere of bitterness. The only comfort she had was the memory of the look on his face just before she had collapsed. Surely he couldn't have looked so agonised if he hadn't cared, even a little. But he had made no attempt to accompany her back to Merida from Ixtlacan, nor had his name been on any of the messages that arrived at the hospital during her short stay.

Was it as simple as that? she wondered sadly. Could you just close off those parts of your life that spelled warmth and desire and hope as soon as they became inconvenient? If she had not been James' wife, but simply a working photographer on an assignment, would Shaun have become her lover for the duration of the trip, and waved her goodbye at the airport when it was over without a second thought?

She took a taxi to the flat, and let herself in quietly. The blinds were drawn at most of the windows, and the air smelt stale and used. Gabrielle whisked round, pulling back curtains and struggling with stiff sash cords. She took the dust sheets off most of the furniture in the sitting room and folded them neatly, stowing them in one of the bedrooms for the time being. Then she went into the kitchen. None of the mains services had been disconnected, and she filled the kettle and found an unopened jar of coffee. Unless the unknown expert liked his coffee black, she would need to get some milk from somewhere. There were no shops nearby, but there were people in the adjoining flats. Surely someone would give her a drop of milk. She took a small jug from the kitchen cabinet, and left the flat leaving the front door slightly ajar. Her immediate neighbours were out, but the woman who lived in the flat opposite answered her rather tentative ring. Gabrielle introduced herself with some diffidence. James had never made the slightest attempt as far as she could gather to get to know any of the neighbours, and she could imagine how he would have reacted to a suggestion that they might borrow something as trivial as a jug of milk from one of them. But Mrs Appleforth proved a pleasant woman, and she greeted Gabrielle with real warmth.

'I was so sorry to read about Dr Warner,' she remarked, leading the way into her gay yellow and white kitchen. 'I don't think many of us had realised quite what a distinguished career he'd had until the obituary appeared.'

She saw Gabrielle looking at her with raised brows. 'The obituary in *The Times*, my dear. I thought as his widow, you would have been responsible . . .'

Gabrielle shook her head. 'I'm afraid I was rather ill

following my husband's death,' she said quietly. 'I wasn't aware of very much at all, and I don't suppose anyone bothered to mention it to me.'

'No.' Mrs Appleforth bit her lip. 'Perhaps I shouldn't have mentioned it, but . . .'

'Oh, no,' Gabrielle assured her. 'I—I'm fine now. I'd been under a lot of stress, you see.'

'Someone told me that you'd actually been in the Yucatan with Dr Warner.' Mrs Appleforth gave a little shudder. 'I think you must be incredibly brave. All those unpleasant things dropping on one out of the trees! I expect you're very glad to be back in civilisation.' She handed Gabrielle the jug of milk.

'It has its points,' Gabrielle conceded, looking with some amusement at the automatic dishwasher, and recalling the primitive arrangements in operation at Ixtlacan. 'But so, believe it or not, has the rain forest.'

'Surely you wouldn't go back?' Mrs Appleforth looked her over, taking in the long-sleeved cream bouclé dress, the tall suede boots, and the mass of curling hair, confined at the nape of her neck by a bronze clip. 'So many painful memories for you.'

As she carried the milk back to the flat, Gabrielle wondered ruefully what Mrs Appleforth would have said if she had told her that most of her painful memories were tied up in this very building.

As she got to the front door, she saw that it was now wide open and guessed that her visitor had arrived. She went into the hall and glimpsed a man's tall figure in the sitting room.

'I'm sorry,' she apologised, pushing open the door. 'I hope you haven't been waiting long . . .'

She gave a choked cry as her eyes met Shaun's and the jug fell from her hand, cascading milk down her dress and on to the carpet.

'Leave it,' he ordered brusquely, seeing that she was

about to go down on her knees to clear up the mess. 'There's broken china. You'll hurt yourself.'

He was probably right, she thought hysterically as he helped her to her feet. Her hands were shaking so much she might have cut a main artery.

'Here, sit down.' He pushed her down on to the sofa and pushed a clean handkerchief into her hand. 'Mop your dress with this.'

'The milk was for your coffee,' she said lamely. 'I'll have to go and ask her for some more. She'll think I'm mad.'

'Be still,' he said roughly. 'You don't think I've come all this way to sit and drink bloody coffee, do you?'

'Why have you come?' She scrubbed furiously and unavailingly at the front of her dress.

'Don't you know?' he said quietly.

'Of course—the Institute sent you.' She did not look at him. 'I had a letter just this morning. They said they would be sending someone to advise me. But I—I didn't expect it would be you.'

'No,' he said drily, 'I don't suppose you did at that. But you must have known I'd come sooner or later.'

'Must I?' she said, past the constriction in her throat.

He looked taller than ever in a dark suit, the elegance of his white silk shirt set off by a dark red tie. She thought of the last time she had seen him, tired and unshaven, his clothes stained with blood from attending to James' wound. There could hardly have been a greater contrast.

'I told myself I ought to wait a decent interval—only I couldn't find anyone to tell me how long that should be.' He took out a cheroot and lit it reflectively. 'Whatever it is, it's too long. I found it totally unbearable.'

He looked at her. 'You look like hell. How much weight have you lost? And why those shadows under your eyes?'

'I haven't been sleeping too well,' she said unevenly.

'Do you suppose I have?' He swung round and sent the

partly smoked cheroot flying violently into the empty fireplace.

Gabrielle shook her head helplessly. 'I think we'd better make a start on the inventory,' she said in a low voice. 'There's some paper in James' study. I'll fetch it.'

'Later.' He caught at her arm, compelling her to stand still. His nearness was like a drug. Pride fought with need within her, and need won. 'You've been fretting,' he said abruptly. 'Why? Surely not for James?'

'Would that be so extraordinary?' She kept her eyes lowered, frightened that he would read the truth in them. 'I was married to him, after all.'

'Oh, yes, a ceremony did take place—I'm aware of that. But as you've already admitted to me, there wasn't a great deal more to the relationship than the actual ceremony. And James' own attitude to you confirmed that.' His lips twisted derisively as she looked up at him bewilderedly. 'Don't pretend, Gabrielle. James didn't even know who you were—he thought you were married to me at one point. Told me "my wife" was a "sweet child". And it wasn't you he called for at the end, either. You know that, don't you?'

'Yes,' she said with difficulty. 'Please—can we get on with the inventory? I—I do have other things to do today and . . .'

'Name one.' He was standing so close to her that their bodies were almost touching. She closed her eyes and made herself step back, away from him.

'Why did it have to be you?' she said almost inaudibly.

'Because I was in London—at the Institute when your letter arrived, and because I have, let's say, a vested interest in the items stored in this flat.'

'Of course. Most of them have been taken from sites that you hoped to excavate yourself.'

'That's part of it. Aren't you going to ask why I didn't contact you before?'

'It's none of my business how you spend your time.'

God, she sounded so prim! He was laughing, and no wonder.

'What incredible self-control,' he mocked. 'I thought curiosity was an essential part of any woman's make-up. But you're wrong, anyway, because some of it is very much your business. I went to see Martin Gilbert at *Vision* yesterday. I had some photographs and a script to deliver. I was told to tell you he's delighted with them both.'

Gabrielle realised she had totally forgotten the films of the early part of the expedition that she had sent to the processing laboratories in Merida. Aunt Molly had contacted *Vision*, she knew, to explain that she had been unable to complete the assignment because of her breakdown, and Martin Gilbert had written to her conveying his sympathy and hoping that she would contact him when she was well again.

'All he's waiting for now are some shots of the jade mask, and the gold necklaces and ornaments that we—rescued from Ixtlacan.'

'Gold?' she questioned faintly.

Shaun nodded. 'Exquisite stuff, and in fine condition. Craig spent days piecing the mask together too. It's all waiting for you.'

'No.' She shook her head. 'I—I can't ... You'll have to get someone else.'

'Why not you?'

'You of all people should be able to answer that,' she accused him, sudden colour flaring in her cheeks. 'How can I face them—Anna and the others, now that everyone knows about James?'

'All that's happened is that suspicion has become certainty. No one believes you had any part in it, or blames you in any way.'

'Except you.'

'If I still thought that,' he said slowly, 'do you imagine for one minute that I'd be within a hundred miles of you?'

'I don't know what to think,' she said wearily. 'You made it very clear in the past that you wanted nothing more to do with me.'

'If that's the impression I gave, I deserve an Oscar,' he said drily. 'Like you, I didn't know what to think. All the evidence suggested you were a cheap, conniving gold-digger of the worst kind, yet my senses told me a totally different story. Perhaps I should have listened to them more.'

'Perhaps,' she said with difficulty. 'I—I'll go and make that coffee.'

He looked at her sharply. 'You really can't bear to be alone with me, can you? Make your damned coffee, then, if it will make you feel any better.'

While she made the coffee, he disposed of the pieces of broken jug, and wiped the carpet with a damp cloth.

'Give me the tray.' He came to stand at her side. 'We don't want another accident.'

She followed him back into the sitting room, and accepted the cup he handed to her.

'What now?' He sat down on one of the armchairs. 'Do we make polite conversation or can we talk—really talk?'

'We have nothing to say to each other.' She took a sip of the black and scalding brew in her cup and winced slightly.

'I don't agree.' He leaned back in the chair, very much at ease. 'After I left *Vision* I went to call on Elaine.'

Gabrielle gasped, and set the cup down with trembling fingers.

'I'm glad to see I get some reaction at last.' His voice was cool and speculative.

'What—is she like?' she asked rather faintly.

He shrugged. 'Red-haired—green-eyed. She could be your mother—or your very much older sister. But there the resemblance ends. She's married again—a very rich man, and doing very well, thank you. I was prepared to loathe her, but in the end I couldn't.'

He stared down at the carpet and frowned. 'I told her about James—naturally. She said all the right things, but I could tell that none of it was any real surprise to her. So I questioned her a little. She said that James had an obsession about other men from the day they were married, and that nothing she could say or do could reassure him. At first she used to ask him about his work, but he used to accuse her of being more interested in the other archaeologists than she was in the dig, so she stopped asking. When he was at home, she couldn't stir out of the flat without a full-scale inquisition.' He paused. 'He would never discuss financial matters with her. She had no idea what his salary was. All she knew was that he was often extremely generous—sometimes preposterously so, and she became worried. The more she questioned him, the worse things got. Eventually he told her what he'd become involved in. I think she was genuinely horrified. It was about this time that he started begging her not to leave him.'

'But she did leave him.'

'Yes. She claims in order to bring him to his senses—shock treatment. Then she found she was being divorced for desertion. She tried to see him, to discuss the matter, but he refused even to communicate with her by letter.'

Gabrielle stared at him. 'But if he divorced her, why did he behave as if the marriage had never ended—confuse me with her?'

Shaun shrugged quietly. 'As Elaine said, he was obsessed. I think he fed this obsession for the rest of his life.'

Gabrielle's hands twisted together. 'And I did nothing.'

'What could you have done?' His voice hardened.

'Surely I could have helped. If I'd been different. I—I didn't love James when I married him—not as I should have done—I know that now . . .' She paused, flushing at that piece of self-betrayal, but if Shaun was aware of it, he gave no sign.

'I don't think it made any difference at all. I believe James married you because you looked like his first wife. While he kept you at a distance, he could maintain the fiction, convince himself that she had returned to him—justify everything he had done. Any real intimacy between you, and the whole fantasy would have collapsed like a house of cards.' He rose to his feet and came over to her. 'We all knew James was married,' he told her quietly. 'A few—Grace Morgan for one—knew that his marriage had been through difficulties. You were—quite a shock when you appeared. Dennis suspected the truth when he saw the date on your marriage certificate. You'd only been married a matter of months, and James'—problems had begun several years before. Dennis was on your side almost from the start, and that's why you came to Ixtlacan with us.'

'But you were against me from the first.' She got up and walked restlessly over to the window.

'Was I?' He followed her, standing behind her. His breath was warm on her hair. 'All I knew was that I wanted you, desperately, almost from the first moment I saw you. But I fought it—God, did I fight it! No woman was going to do to me what had been done to Warner—I'd sworn that. And then I found I'd fallen in love with the same woman.' He laughed, savagely. 'Ironic, wasn't it? I nearly went insane. All the time, I was trying to despise you—trying to prove you were the tramp that I believed. And yet at the same time I knew that if I was separated from you, I'd bleed to death. When Warner died, calling for Elaine, it was like the answer to a prayer. I came to find you—to apologise to you on my knees if necessary—and you know what I found.' His hands came up and clasped her shoulders. 'I couldn't live with myself after you went back to Merida,' he said in a low voice. 'I told myself that your illness was all my fault. That I'd driven you to it—that I should have obeyed all my instincts and believed in your innocence from the start.' Gently he turned her to face him. 'Coming here this morning, I was frightened,' he said. 'Frightened that I might make you ill again—or that I'd made you hate me and you'd send me away. Have I ruined everything for us, Gabrielle, or can you forgive me and let me try and make up for all the hard things I've said and done?'

'I told you once that I wanted you to love me—in all the ways there were.' Her voice trembled. 'I still want that, Shaun. I've never stopped loving you. I don't think I could, no matter what you did . . .'

His mouth silenced her. She clung to him, unashamedly returning passion for passion, every inch of her body vibrant with response under his caressing hands. They were both breathless when the kiss ended.

'Now you'll have to marry me.' His voice was husky with desire, but his eyes glinted wickedly at her. 'I have to be back in Ixtlacan at the end of the week, so the only honeymoon hotel I can offer you is the Temple of the Moon.'

'The end of the week!' she gasped. 'But, Shaun, we can't. What will people say?'

'I don't even care.' He drew her back into his arms, moulding her slender body against his. 'But it won't come as any great surprise to Anna or any of the others. I must have been impossible to live with just lately.'

'What's so unusual about that?' She gave a mock sigh, her eyes lingering over the new tenderness softening the dark arrogance of his face. 'What am I letting myself in for?'

'I'd be happy to demonstrate.' He bent his head, parting her lips with his with devastating mastery.

'You said you wanted to be loved in all the ways there were,' he whispered, against her mouth. 'Well, this is only the first . . .'